BOUGHT FOR REVENGE, BEDDED FOR PLEASURE

BOUGHT FOR REVENGE, BEDDED FOR PLEASURE

BY

EMMA DARCY

MILLS & BOON®

Pure reading pleasure™

First published in Great Britain 2008
Large Print edition 2008
Harlequin Mills & Boon Limited,
Eton House, 18-24 Paradise Road,
Richmond, Surrey TW9 1SR

© Emma Darcy 2008

ISBN: 978 0 263 20090 4

Set in Times Roman 16¾ on 19 pt.
16-1108-46278

Printed and bound in Great Britain
by CPI Antony Rowe, Chippenham, Wiltshire

PROLOGUE

"I'm JACK MAGUIRE, Leonard Maguire's son," he told the man on the other side of the security gate, feeling the bitter irony of having his identity questioned.

"Didn't know he had one," the man muttered, a frown beetling over suspicious eyes. "You've got an American accent."

Hardly surprising since Jack had been tucked away, living in Texas for most of his growing-up years. But he'd been born in Australia, a seven-year-old boy when he'd been taken from this country. Now, at twenty-four, he was a man—a man of means, he thought with intense satisfaction—and ready to make his mark on his father's home ground.

"Just call the house and check me out," he instructed.

While the security guard did just that, using a mobile 'phone he'd detached from his belt, Jack's gaze travelled up the long avenue of maples which led to the huge sprawling house at the top of the hill overlooking the valley. It was spring and the new leaves on the trees were a brilliant lime green in the bright afternoon sunshine. The whole valley was green—prime property—nothing but the best for his father's second family.

The house was white. The fences were white. Everything kept in a pristine state. Which, of course, cost a lot of money. *A lot.* Which was only to be expected of a man who owned a vast transport company, including a domestic airline. All Jack had ever got from him were birthday cards, Christmas cards—probably sent by whoever his current secretary was—and a few days at a luxury hotel in Las Vegas when his father was there on business, once when Jack was twelve and again when he was eighteen.

He remembered being asked that last time, "What do you intend to do with your life, boy?"

As though it had nothing to do with Leonard Maguire.

Still, Jack had asked hopefully, "Are you offering an opportunity?"

Any such idea was totally obliterated by the harsh reply. "No. Make your own way, as I did. If you have the guts to do it you'll become a man I can respect."

The challenge had eaten into Jack's soul. His father was a self-made billionaire, starting from nothing, building a transport empire. Yet looking at the evidence of his wealth now— wealth spent freely on his second wife and two adopted daughters—Jack could feel no respect for him. What kind of man did nothing for his flesh-and-blood son and gave every privilege money could provide to a couple of girls his second wife had wanted and acquired? Would *they* be told to make their own way when they were eighteen?

The security man clicked his 'phone shut and gave Jack a look of curious sympathy. "Can't let you in, mate. I've been told to run you off. Lady Ellen says you're not welcome here."

Lady Ellen. The title soured Jack's stomach. She'd been an on-the-make young office clerk, sleeping with her much older boss, committing adultery, and now because his father had been knighted for services to his country and she was his wife, she could call herself *Lady.*

"Ask to speak to my father," he demanded.

"No can do. Sir Leonard is not home yet."

"When does he arrive home?"

"Helicopter usually flies in about seven." The man glanced at his watch. "Another three hours from now. No sense in waiting around. Can't let you past the gate unless I get the word."

Jack had got the message. His father's home was forbidden territory to him as far as Lady Ellen was concerned. Probably always had been. Bitch, guarding her own interests tooth and nail. Though his father hadn't bucked them.

How much power did she wield over her much-older husband? Whose choice was it to keep *the son* in exile?

There was so much Jack wanted to know.

Was determined to know.

"I'll be back," he said.

"I'm stationed in the cottage," the guard warned, nodding to the small ranch house overlooking the entrance to the property.

He was making it clear that no one slipped past him. The guy was probably in his early fifties but his big, burly frame was still all muscle—a formidable opponent in a fight. Not that Jack was looking for one, not with this man, who was just doing his job. He returned to the rental car he'd hired at the airport, thinking the view from the ranch house did not take in the whole perimeter of this estate.

Half an hour later he'd parked the car on the verge of a side road, raided his luggage for jeans, a dark-blue T-shirt, and Nikes, changed out of his visiting clothes and hiked cross-country to the white fence that marked the territory he wanted to scout.

He leaned on the top railing for a while, taking in the view of horses grazing in lush pastures, what was undoubtedly state-of-the-art stables, and a rider—a girl with a mass of red-gold curls streaming out from the tight constriction of her riding hat—putting her horse through a series of pony club jumps.

Was she the elder of the two adopted daughters?

Or a stable hand, employed to train the horse to jumping?

The slender figure looked shapely enough to be a young woman, though that factor certainly didn't rule out a girl of fourteen. She rode well, handling the horse with confident authority, but then he had, too, at fourteen, having learnt the hard way on his stepfather's ranch.

He scaled the fence and strolled towards the exercise enclosure, wanting his curiosity satisfied. It was a matter of supreme indifference to him that he was trespassing. To his mind he

had more natural right to be here than anyone else on this property.

Sally didn't see the man's approach. Blaze
hadn't been completely set right for the triple
jump and she wanted to take him through it
again. The big gelding had been too eager. She
had to rein him in a bit, make the timing perfect.
Her concentration on the task was total. Only
when Blaze had sailed beautifully over the third
hurdle did the sound of clapping alert her to the
presence of a spectator.

Flushed and exhilarated by her success, she
turned to smile at the person who had admired
her skill enough to applaud it, expecting to see
Tim Fogarty, the stable hand who always helped
her groom Blaze for showjumping. It startled
her to see a stranger, especially a stranger who
was alone. That didn't happen here. A visitor
was always accompanied by someone.

He was very handsome, outstandingly so
compared to the young men of her acquain-

tance—thick black hair, a face that instantly drew fascinated interest, and his tall and strong physique was definitely ten out of ten. His forearms, resting on the top railing of the enclosure, were tanned and muscular, suggesting he lived an outdoors life. Maybe he was a new employee.

Sally nudged Blaze into walking over to where the man stood, aware that the flutter in her stomach was caused more by a sense of excitement than curiosity. His eyes were examining her in a very detailed fashion—vivid blue eyes—making her extremely conscious of how she looked and raising a silly hope that he found her attractive.

It *was* silly because it was obvious he was too old for her. In his twenties, she judged. At fourteen she had the height and the figure of a young woman but not the years to match this man. There was something in his eyes—a knowingness that came from a lot of hard learnt experience.

"Who are you?" she asked, feeling a compulsion to learn everything she could about him.

His mouth quirked into a dryly amused little smile, making her wonder how it would feel to have such beautifully sculptured lips kissing hers. Would they be gentle and sensitive to her response or hard and ravishing? He was the kind of man who could have stepped out of one of the romance books she'd read, making her wish for things that weren't yet part of her life.

"Who are you?" he countered, surprising her with his American accent. Nice voice, though, deep and manly.

"I'm Sally Maguire," she answered with a touch of pride, wanting to impress him with her status as daughter to a man who was virtually an Australian legend.

"Ah…" he said, but it wasn't an admiring *Ah,* more a mocking one that told her he wasn't impressed at all.

Had she seemed snobby about who she was?

"Fine horse," he remarked. "You handle him well. Have you been riding long?"

She nodded, suddenly feeling ill at ease with him. "Dad gave me a pony when I was five."

"No doubt he bought this one for you, too."

The mocking tone was more pronounced this time.

"Who are you?" she repeated more sharply. "What are you doing here?"

He shrugged. "Just looking around."

"This is private property. If you have no business here, you're trespassing."

"Oh, I have business to be done. Very personal business." His eyes stabbed into hers like blue lasers, scouring her soul. "I'm waiting for my father to come home."

None of the employees had a son like him. She was sure of it. "Who's your father?"

"The same as yours."

Shock rendered her speechless for a moment. Was it true? A bastard son who'd never been publicly acknowledged? He didn't look like her father, though he did have blue eyes, a much sharper blue though.

"I know nothing about you," she blurted out, seized by the fear that whoever he was, he'd come to make trouble.

"Not surprising," he drawled derisively. "I'm sure Lady Ellen prefers to pretend I don't exist."

He hated her mother. She could see it, hear it, feel it.

"She probably doesn't know about you, either," Sally threw at him defensively, fretting over his attitude.

He shook his head. "What a protected little cocoon you live in, Sally Maguire!" There was a wicked challenge in his eyes as he added, "Why don't you ask Lady Ellen about the marriage she busted up and the boy she wanted no part of?"

"What marriage?"

"Leonard Maguire's marriage to *my* mother," he tossed at her, obviously confident that he was dealing with irrefutable fact.

Sally could only stare at him, her mind struggling to take this stunning information on board. If what he said was true, he wasn't a bastard son. He was her father's natural-born heir, not adopted like her and her younger sister. Her very safe world suddenly felt very shaken.

"Have you been up to the house?" she asked in a burst of panic, feeling that everything she'd thought she'd known was about to change.

"Not yet."

"Does my mother know you're here?"

"She knows I've come. Lady Ellen was not inclined to put out the welcome mat for me. In fact, she had me turned away at the gate. What do you think of that, Sally Maguire?" He cocked his head to one side, mockingly assessing her reaction to this information. "Here you are on prime horseflesh, revelling in having your love of riding indulged and completely catered for—" he gestured towards the stables, obvious evidence for his viewpoint "—and *I* am turned away from setting foot on my father's land."

It wasn't fair.

It wasn't right.

A sense of guilty shame sent a gush of heat flooding into her cheeks. Yet she had only this man's word that what he was telling her was true. She had no idea of what had happened with these relationships in the past, before she was born and adopted into this family. Maybe her mother had good reason to block his entry to this property. Hadn't she just felt her own world being threatened by him?

"What do you want?" The words spilled out of the fear that was curdling her stomach. He wouldn't have come if he didn't *want* something.

"I had my father for seven years. You've had him for fourteen. Wouldn't you say there should be a better balance to be struck?"

"Like what? You're grown up now. There's no way of getting back years that are gone," she argued anxiously. He knew her age. It felt all wrong that he had information about her and she had none about him.

"True," he agreed. His eyes went flint hard. "But there's the future to be reckoned with."

He *was* going to make trouble. "What about *your* mother?" Sally threw at him, trying to mitigate the situation he'd spelled out. "She must have taken you with her. Where is she now?"

"Dead," he stated bluntly, his voice flat, showing no emotion at all.

Somehow that was more frightening than anything else. "I'm sorry," she said defensively. "Sorry you feel—" Her mind sought frantically for the right word "—displaced."

Which was what she would have felt if she hadn't been adopted. Having no parents, no sense of belonging to a family…it would be awful, an empty life. She'd been so lucky, while he…

"I wasn't displaced," he corrected her savagely. "I was *replaced* by you and the other adopted daughter."

"I didn't know. Jane doesn't know, either," she pleaded.

It wasn't her fault. Yet he was making her feel horribly guilty.

"I'll go and talk to my mother," she offered, feeling too churned up to stay talking to him, and needing to know why he had been turned away.

"That should be an interesting conversation," he mocked. "Pity I can't be a fly on the wall."

The taunt spurred her into nudging Blaze into a canter. She rode quickly to the exit from the enclosure, intensely conscious of those laser-blue eyes boring into her. Forced to pause while opening the gate, she couldn't stop herself from looking back at him. He hadn't moved. His gaze *was* fixed on her. It felt hard, relentless, accusing.

"You haven't told me your name," she called out, wishing he could be more…brotherly.

"It's Maguire," he reminded her with derisive emphasis. "Jack Maguire. Commonly known as Blackjack in some circles. It's a name that darkens other people's dreams."

It was a name that would haunt Sally for a long time to come. Ten years would pass before she would meet him again—ten years before he would once more set foot on this land, bringing with him the bitter harvest of the wrongs that were being enacted today.

Jack watched her go. She didn't stable her horse. She galloped straight up the hill as though the hounds of hell were at her heels. The sun was starting to set, burning the clouds in the sky, spreading a haze of red around the big white house. He hoped Sally Maguire would spread some heartburn around with her questions about him.

Time to return to his car, leave this property before Lady Ellen sent a posse to run him off. He probably shouldn't have said so much to the girl, venting his anger at how he'd been treated, but the urge to set a cat amongst the pigeons had been irresistible.

And she was so damned beautiful, he'd wanted to claw her off her complacent perch, make her aware of a darker side to her world of privilege.

He'd revelled in the troubled worry reflected in her fascinating sage-green eyes, in the scarlet flush that had stained her flawless, pale skin.

She'd been given too much and he'd been given too little.

That was the core of it.

He'd come on a scouting mission to feel out the lay of the land. Once he knew precisely what he was dealing with, he'd work out how to achieve what he wanted.

One certainty burned in his mind.

Whatever it took, somehow, some day, the scales would be balanced.

CHAPTER ONE

Ten Years On...

SALLY stared at the coffin which held her father.
It was still difficult to believe he was dead, that
a sudden fatal heart attack could steal his life
away. No warning. Never a day's illness that she
knew of. He'd always radiated such a powerful
life force, the shock of its being ended so
abruptly was still numbing any sense of grief.
Which was just as well since her mother had instructed her and Jane to maintain absolute
dignity during this funeral service.

They were on public show.

They had to do their father proud.

Sir Leonard Maguire was being honoured today.

There'd been television crews outside the cathedral, shooting their arrival, not to mention all the powerful people who'd come to pay their last respects: politicians, captains of industry, the horseracing fraternity. She could hear them taking their places behind her, shuffling into the pews, greeting each other in muffled tones.

On the other side of the aisle were the major figures in her father's work force—his other family—who had shared his dreams of a transport empire and been closely involved in carrying out his grand plans. He'd spent much more time with them than with us, Sally thought. They were probably devastated by his death, not only grieving for their leader but wondering what would come next. Who would fill the huge shoes of the man who was no longer with them?

She had no grasp of her father's business. Neither did Jane who was studying to become a nurse. Her mother had dedicated her life to being the perfect wife, certainly the CEO of their home, but not interested in anything beyond maintaining the social status that was all important to her. They'd been cocooned in the protection of great wealth, but none of them knew what would happen now. They were floating in a vacuum.

Maybe her father had provided the answers in his will. Tomorrow they had to go to the solicitor's office to hear it read. Her mother was upset—furious—that Victor Newell, who'd been her father's legal advisor for many years, had refused to come to them in the privacy and comfort of their own home. It meant another trip to the city, another brave front to be put on in public.

Regardless of being subjected to her mother's intense displeasure over the telephone, the solicitor had not budged from his edict, stating he was following Sir Leonard's instructions. No argument prevailed against that. Not even her mother could break her father's iron grip on the people he had employed.

But he'd lost his grip on life. No, he'd had it taken from him. Probably the only thing that had ever been taken from him. Except…

The memory of Jack Maguire flashed into her mind. Despite what her parents had told her, she didn't really believe his mother had taken him from the man who now lay in this coffin. Her father had chosen to let him go. She couldn't imagine anything else, especially since he'd chosen not to have him back. It was the only reasonable answer to why Jack Maguire had not become part of their lives.

Too late now for the scales to be balanced, she thought sadly.

He'd made such a strong impact on her at their one and only meeting, she'd often wondered how he'd dealt with his father's rejection. It would surely have bitten deep. Though that personal blow had not stopped him from becoming a successful business entrepreneur in his own right. Maybe it had spurred him on to make a name for himself.

She'd read about him in the newspapers from time to time, fixing deals that were highly profitable. Photographs of him never showed him smiling, not even when he was pictured with beautiful women at A-list parties. His eyes were always cold. She'd imagined it was because his heart was cold, no family to warm it.

No chance left of its ever being warmed by acceptance or approval from his father. The media had given enormous coverage to Sir Leonard Maguire's life and death in the past few days so he would certainly know about it. Jack had been mentioned as *the estranged son.* Such a cold phrase. It had made her feel bad again about being a much-indulged adopted daughter.

The organ music droned to a halt. Sally glanced at her watch. It was time for the funeral service to begin. The Bishop of Sydney would emerge from the vestry any moment now, ready to conduct the ceremony. The congregation hushed. The footsteps of a latecomer walking down the aisle were clearly audible, not hurrying, measured at a dignified pace. Whoever it was seemed to have an unsettling presence, giving rise to a rush of whispering. The footsteps kept coming, right up to the front pew.

Was it the bishop, making some kind of ceremonial arrival? Out of the corner of her eye, Sally saw her mother's head turn slightly— licence enough to take a sideways glance without being reprimanded since her mother was doing the same thing.

It was a man in a black suit, royal-blue shirt. He'd paused in the middle of the aisle, right beside them, and from the hiss of her mother's sharply indrawn breath, he was someone who did not meet with her approval. Sally instinctively leaned forward to see his face, wanting to identify the problem.

Shock knifed through her.

Jack Maguire!

His strikingly handsome face was grimly set, a cold blue gaze projecting hostile scorn at her mother, whose head jerked forward, instantly breaking whatever eye contact he'd drawn from her. His mouth curled mockingly as his gaze slid to Sally who was too stunned by his presence to do anything but stare openly at him.

For a moment he stared back and she felt herself beginning to burn, heat surging into her cheeks. He nodded, as though she'd given him the reaction he wanted, then turned away, moving to the front pew on the other side of the aisle, seating himself directly opposite her mother, where amazingly there was a place vacant for him and none of her father's top executives queried his right to take it.

He *was* Sir Leonard Maguire's son.

Did they think he might be his heir?

It made no sense to Sally. The estrangement had been total…hadn't it?

Strike one! Jack thought with intense satisfaction. The shock and chagrin on Lady Ellen's face was worth his own bit of stage management. The gall of the woman, writing him a letter to say he wasn't welcome at Sir Leonard's funeral. He hoped his prominent presence here would eat into her mean heart and destroy her arrogant composure.

Sitting there in fashion-plate perfection, the stylish black hat framing artfully streaked honey-blonde hair, big brown eyes subtly shaded to look mournful, pearls around her throat, a black suit—no doubt carrying a designer label—hugging her voluptuous figure. She had to be forty-five, but living a life of luxury no doubt contributed to her looking only about thirty. The eighteen-year-old nymphet who'd seduced his father had done very well for herself.

Not so well in the future, Jack vowed.

They made a striking trio, the Maguire women; the blonde, the redhead and the brunette. He'd only caught a glimpse of Jane, sitting beyond Sally in the pew. Dark hair, dark eyes, olive skin, all shadowed by her older sister's blazing beauty, which was far more pronounced now than when she was fourteen. The glorious cascade of red-gold curls, the white skin, still prone to revealing rushes of emotion, the fascinating sage-green eyes… Jack had to admit the woman she was now stirred the beast in him.

He'd like to have her in his bed.

Maybe he'd get her there…one way or another.

The idea had huge appeal, for many reasons.

Sally didn't hear much of the funeral service. Her mind kept circling around Jack Maguire's presence. What did it mean? Had he simply come to see his father buried, taking some dark satisfaction in publicly claiming the relationship that had never been acknowledged to his satisfaction in life, putting any hope of it to bed, once and for all? A funeral was about finality, letting go.

Her mother's hands were not folded neatly on her lap. They were tightly clenched. No way would she make a public scene about Jack Maguire's effrontery in doing what he'd done here in the cathedral, but she was fuming over it. No doubt she'd throw one of her vicious tantrums when they got home. It invariably happened when things didn't go to plan. Everything always had to be picture perfect for her mother, and Jack Maguire was a huge black blot on this landscape.

Blackjack...darkening other people's dreams.

He'd darkened hers, many a time. She'd never been able to forget him. The knowledge that he was out there somewhere, not getting what she got from her father, always ate at her comfort zone about accepting all she did from her parents.

He was not out there today.

He was right here.

Assaulting everyone's comfort zone.

Hymns were sung, prayers recited, eulogies given, the service proceeding as planned, until it was time for them to stand and follow the coffin as it was wheeled out of the cathedral. Her mother stepped out of the pew first. Sally and Jane were supposed to flank her for the walk down the aisle. Before they could take their places, Jack Maguire moved out from his pew, positioning himself beside his father's widow, leaving them no option but to pair up behind them.

For several tense moments—Sally thought her mother might explode at this spoiling intrusion—Lady Ellen stood rigidly still. Jane felt the danger, too, instinctively grabbing Sally's hand for sisterly support. She had always been timid, too scared of horses to ever try riding, and too easily browbeaten by their mother who could be truly scary when she flew out of control. Which didn't happen often. It had never happened in front of their father. But if things didn't go as she planned, as she expected...

Lady Ellen started walking, head held high, determinedly ignoring the man accompanying her. Both Sally and Jane breathed a sigh of relief and followed, keeping pace with the lead couple. Not that they were a couple, Sally thought, not by any stretch of imagination. Her mother and Jack Maguire were two separate units, and the sense they were heading towards a nasty collision had her own nerves twitching and her heart at a gallop.

She studied the back of Jack Maguire's head, fiercely wishing she could see into the workings of his brain. He had pulled back from making trouble ten years ago and kept away from the family, but whatever embargo he must have accepted during that time had obviously been lifted by his father's death. Sally could almost smell trouble in the air, positively sulphurous now for having been held back for so long.

They moved beyond the last pew, beyond ears that might hear.

"Didn't you get my letter, telling you not to come to the funeral?" her mother sliced at Jack Maguire in a low, venomous tone.

"Did you really expect me to respect *your* wishes, Lady Ellen?" he drawled *sotto voce,* the words dripping with derision.

"Your father wouldn't have wanted it."

"My father is beyond speaking for himself."

"He didn't want you with him all these years."

"On the contrary, we lunched regularly together. *You* were kept out of our relationship."

Sally tensed, her mind bombarded by one shock after another, and nervously aware that her mother's supposedly unassailable stance had just been seriously undermined. How would she react to this claim?

"I don't believe you." Flat denial.

"Ask his secretary. She made the appointments," came the mocking reply. "Or any one of his executive staff, all of whom are well aware of the connection."

It certainly answered why the seat in the front pew had been vacant for him! Besides, he spoke with such confidence, Sally could not disbelieve him. And, in her heart of hearts, she was glad he had managed to strike up a relationship with his father, even if it did make her mother furious. All these years of having been shut out from the family had not been right.

They emerged from the cathedral. The funeral attendants lifted the coffin from the trolley to carry it down the steps to the waiting hearse. During the pause while this procedure got underway, they stood in silence, the heat of the midsummer afternoon beating down on them.

Sally wondered what was steaming through her mother's mind. The loss of authority would certainly make her burn, yet she should concede Jack Maguire's right to be here. It was the gracious thing to do. Besides, she couldn't make him go away. This man was not about to bend to her will. He was not of the same breed as the highly civilised, born-to-wealth bachelors her mother kept pushing at her and Jane; more a dark, dangerous animal, primed to pounce.

A little shiver ran down her spine.

Fear or excitement?

She wasn't sure.

Would he speak to her when they moved down to stand behind the hearse? She wanted him to. She *wanted* a connection with him. Though that was an unlikely outcome, given the circumstances.

Obviously he had conceded to his father's wish to keep the family separated during his lifetime, and although that time was now gone, Jack Maguire had no reason to care about the feelings of people who'd never shown any caring for his. Writing him a letter to say he wasn't welcome at his own father's funeral must have been like a red rag to a bull.

"Please have the decency to leave," her mother hissed at him.

"I think the more decent thing is for me to be here, Lady Ellen," he coolly replied.

"You don't belong with us." Spoken more vehemently as the funeral attendants moved beyond close earshot.

"True. But today belongs to my father," he retorted pointedly. "Not you and your daughters."

"We had more of him than you did," she shot back in a flare of temper.

Sally caught a glimpse of icy contempt on his face as he replied, "Well, I hope you stored up a treasure-house of memories, because that's all the treasure you're going to get."

"What do you mean by that?"

He disdained an answer, moving forward to begin descending the steps to the sidewalk.

Her mother hastily followed, grabbing his arm to command his attention. "What do you mean by that?" she repeated, the urgency in her voice revealing deep concern over his last comment.

Sally didn't understand it. Didn't he simply mean that his father was beyond supplying any more memories?

He looked down at the hand clutching him, then directly at his antagonist, raising a sardonic eyebrow. "Do you need my support, Lady Ellen?"

"I do not!" she snapped, instantly removing her hold, tossing her head back and marching on down the steps to the sidewalk.

Jack Maguire strolled after her, not caring about her taking the lead. As she and Jane followed, Sally couldn't help thinking the TV cameras would use this bit of footage for a provocative piece on the widow and the son. And her mother would be furious about that, too, though it was her own fault for losing the control she'd demanded of her daughters.

The four of them stood on the sidewalk together as the coffin was loaded into the hearse and the many floral tributes were arranged around it.

"I will not have you riding in the mourning car with us," her mother warned the man who wouldn't go away at her command.

"I have no intention of mourning with you, Lady Ellen. I really don't care for your company," he stated dryly, then turned his gaze to Sally, the riveting blue eyes intent on capturing and holding her attention.

Her pulse-rate instantly zoomed. It was impossible to look away. Besides which, she didn't want to. He was such a fascinating man, challenging, dangerous, and so good-looking her stomach was all aflutter, registering a strong sexual interest in him, which wasn't sensible at all but well and truly activated nevertheless.

"I must say mourning becomes you, Sally," he

said with an ironic twist. "I've never seen any woman look quite so beautiful at a funeral."

Heat surged through her again. No one had ever called her beautiful, and for *him* to do it...though more likely it was a sly hit at her mother whose beauty invariably did draw comment. For one of her daughters to be viewed as outshining her...yes, he wanted to put her mother down, every way he could.

She could have said she'd never seen any man look quite so handsome—it was the truth—but her mother would have killed her. So she remained silent, her eyes fastened helplessly on his, scarlet cheeks flagging her physical response to the compliment, despite the obvious motive behind it.

"This isn't the time or the place for us to get reacquainted," he went on, addressing her, focussing on her, ignoring her mother. "Perhaps after the meeting at the solicitor's office tomorrow."

"You'll...be...there?"

Sally barely got the words out as her mind

tumbled over the startling news that *he* would be at the reading of the will, and the fact that the solicitor had insisted they come to his office suddenly took on a very ominous meaning. As did Jack's comment to her mother about memories being the only *treasure* she'd be left with. Had her father handed everything over to his son?

"I will most certainly be there." The confirmation was delivered with a cruel little smile, which stayed on his mouth as his glittering blue gaze swept around all three of them. "Until then, ladies."

He walked away.

No, he strode away.

Like a conqueror who'd succeeded in laying waste the enemy, leaving carnage behind him.

The funeral director moved in to usher them to the car for the mourning family. The back door of the hearse had been closed. It was time to go to the cemetery.

Would *he* be there when they arrived?

Sally didn't think so.

Jack Maguire had done what he'd come to do…making his presence felt as a force to be reckoned with and leaving them squirming over what might happen in the solicitor's office tomorrow.

One weight had just been added to the lighter side of the scales.

CHAPTER TWO

ALL the way to the solicitor's office, Sally's mind had been hopelessly torn, her family's needs warring against the natural justice in Jack Maguire's right to be his father's heir.

Her mother, of course, had been railing against the black-sheep son's right to get anything, almost convincing herself that yesterday's scene at the funeral had just been a brazen front, a vengeful slap in the face for denying him a place with the family. There was too much evidence of something very different, Sally thought, but she'd held her tongue, careful not to feed the rage being vented, reducing her sister to a trembling mouse.

"What will we do if he gets it all?" Jane had

asked her fearfully when they'd finally escaped their mother's tirade.

"I don't think that will happen," Sally had answered soothingly.

"But what if it does?"

She'd sighed. "Well, let's face it, Jane. We've been very lucky to have had it good all these years. If our luck runs out, we'll just have to take charge of our own lives instead of being looked after."

Her sister had shaken her head hopelessly. "I'm not strong like you, Sally."

True. Jane had spent her whole life trying to please, seeking approval, happy when she got it, crushed when she didn't. She simply wasn't geared to standing on her own two feet. The training, discipline and determination required to compete successfully on the showjumping circuit had put a lot of steel in Sally's backbone. She knew she wouldn't crumble under adversity. Unfortunately, wishing she could give Jane some of her own steel was futile. Her sister's nature was too different…sweet, gentle and, more often than not, exasperatingly weak.

"Don't worry, Jane. We've been sisters all these years. I won't abandon you, no matter what," she'd said, and then had to mop up a flood of grateful tears.

Abandonment had run through all of Jane's nightmares. Sally had often wondered if it was a common fear of adopted children. She had the same insecurity, which had probably driven her to make the most of all the wonderful opportunities being in the Maguire family had brought her, never quite sure when or if they would be taken away.

There'd always seemed to be a price to be paid for being adopted…dutifully meeting her mother's demands, doing her utmost to hold on to her father's approval. The only unconditional love she'd ever felt was with Jane, even though they weren't blood sisters. Should the privileges they'd been granted come to an end now…well, they'd still have each other.

They were asked to wait in the reception area until Mr. Newell's secretary came to collect them. Her mother interpreted this as VIP service, which put her in a less fractious mood, especially when the secretary, a rather plump woman in her fifties, treated her with great deference as she escorted them into an elevator and poured out sympathy over Sir Leonard's unexpected passing while they rode up to the right floor.

Lady Ellen was responding very graciously to the secretary who ushered them to what looked like a men's club private meeting room. Five dark-green leather chairs were placed around an oval table of highly polished mahogany. Bookshelves full of serious leather tomes lined the walls. An elegant traymobile was set up with various refreshments.

Five chairs. Would the secretary take one of them or was the fifth chair for Jack Maguire? Had he been bluffing about being at this meeting yesterday, giving them a night of worry as a payback for the rotten feelings her mother had undoubtedly inflicted on him with her letter?

The secretary directed them to the three chairs around one end of the table and proceeded to the traymobile, asking for their preferred drinks. Sally and Jane decided on simple glasses of water but their mother went for the whole ceremonial fuss of requesting Earl Grey tea with a slice of lemon. They were all served with little plates of finger sandwiches and dainty pastries. Neither Sally nor Jane felt like eating anything but their mother suddenly found a cheerful appetite. Apparently *she* had decided there was no longer any cause for concern.

Satisfied with her ministering, the secretary excused herself to go and tell Mr. Newell they were waiting for him.

"Will she come back?" Jane whispered anxiously, nodding to the fifth chair.

"I don't know," Sally murmured, nowhere near as sure as her mother that Jack Maguire was out of the picture.

"What are you girls muttering about?" their mother demanded.

Jane instantly shrank back in her chair.

"We're just a bit nervous about what's going to happen next," Sally answered.

"Obviously *we* are the beneficiaries of your father's will." Declared with confidence.

"Yes," Sally quickly agreed. Raising doubts would instantly snap that good humour, so she kept them to herself. Better to keep quiet and simply wait, but she couldn't help feeling tense. Until the fifth chair was occupied by someone else, the spectre of Blackjack Maguire was hanging over it, certainly darkening Jane's dreams.

As for her own…what did she want?

The bottom-line truth was she wanted to see Jack Maguire in that chair even though it meant he was a threat to the life she'd had up until now. She wanted him to get something from his father. It would be wrong if he didn't. But more than anything else she wanted to see him again, wanted to feel the physical thrill of his presence, wanted him to pursue an acquaintance with her as he had suggested yesterday.

It was undoubtedly sheer madness to be craving some involvement with him, given the family history. Her mother would have a fit if she knew. Jane would be frightened for her. Yet the strong tug of the man kept pulling at her mind, her heart. Her whole body buzzed with excitement at the thought of connecting with him. No one else had ever affected her like this.

Maybe it was a dark dream, better set aside.

She'd probably be wiser after this meeting.

If he came.

Her heart leapt as the door to the meeting room opened, but the man who entered was not Jack Maguire. He was tall and lean, meticulously dressed in a dark-grey suit, white shirt, dark-red and grey striped tie, the tip of a matching dark-red handkerchief peaking out of his coat pocket. Sally judged him to be in his fifties, grey hair getting sparse, making his high forehead even higher, rimless spectacles resting on a hawkish nose, narrow jaw, thin lips.

This had to be the solicitor, Victor Newell. She'd never met him but he certainly had the distinguished air of authority that went with heading one of the most reputable legal firms in Sydney—the kind of man who was accustomed to people coming to him, not the other way around.

He gestured to someone still outside in the corridor, and Sally held her breath, wanting it to be Jack Maguire, no matter what that meant.

Yes!

It was him!

A weird exultation bubbled through her.

She told herself she was glad that his father had not disowned him.

But the truth was far more personal than that.

He was here, in the same room as herself, and there was a chance that something might happen between them.

* * *

The moment of truth, Jack thought sardonically, stepping inside and sweeping his gaze around the three women, waiting for the reading of the will.

Lady Ellen had lightened her funeral garb this morning. Her black hat had a white edging around the rim, matching the white edging around the lapels of her suit coat—the stylish *grande dame.* Her eyes flared hatred and her mouth compressed to an unattractive thin line when she saw him.

Jack smiled.

Sally wasn't wearing a hat, her glorious red-gold curls tumbling free, and Jack instantly envisaged them spread in disarray across a pillow. She wore a sage-green linen shirtmaker dress, very prim and proper for this occasion, though the button-through style was quite provocative since he instantly started imagining undoing all her buttons. The colour matched her eyes, which were pinned on him with guarded interest. No thinning of those lush lips. He wondered how she'd respond if he crushed them with his own.

The younger sister looked about to faint with fright, staring at him as though he was the devil himself, complete with horns and pitchfork. Her lips were parted, gasping in air. She wore a beige outfit—no hat—and with her brown hair and brown eyes, seemed totally colourless next to Sally. Jack had the impression Jane wished she could disappear. He actually felt a stab of sympathy for her. Which was absurd. She'd had a good twenty-one years with the Maguire wealth.

"Good morning, all," he said cheerfully, strolling around the table to the chair facing the two sisters.

Sally was the only one who returned the greeting, and promptly flushed when she realised she was on her own in acknowledging his presence. But she didn't shoot an apologetic look at her mother. Her gaze remained fixed on him, a rebellious glint in her eyes.

Excitement fizzed through Jack. She had fire. And backbone. A mind of her own. The idea of pursuing a connection with her grew stronger legs. It had been circling around in his mind since yesterday's funeral service. As perverse as it was of him to find Sally Maguire so desirable, there was no denying the sexual chemistry she'd stirred. He'd wondered if it was because of *who* she was—forbidden territory. It certainly added a piquancy to the attraction. But right now it was pure gut stuff. Everything about her appealed.

He knew this morning's meeting could very well turn him into a hated antagonist in her mind. Any normal man-woman approach to her would be wiped out. But that only made the situation between them even more interesting, challenging, exciting. He needed to get into her mind, find out what was important to her, play on it.

Victor Newell made a little ceremony of greeting each one of them before taking the chair at the head of the table, directly facing Lady Ellen, who obviously took this to mean she was the major player in the will, throwing Jack a snooty, condescending look as though she imagined he was here for a few insignificant crumbs.

The solicitor leaned forward with an earnest air, his hands linked over the manila folder which contained Sir Leonard Maguire's last will and testament. He addressed Lady Ellen.

"Please accept my sympathy over Sir Leonard's passing. I know he expected to live for many more years. It is most unfortunate that his time was cut short."

She nodded with sombre dignity.

Victor sighed and opened the folder. "This will was made and signed a year ago. It's very simple. There are only two beneficiaries. It reads...to my son, Jack Ryan Maguire, I give one dollar..."

"One dollar!" A wild peal of laughter erupted from Lady Ellen's throat. Her eyes danced malicious triumph at Jack. "How brilliant of Leonard! You can't contest his will since he's put you in it."

"I have no intention of contesting it, Lady Ellen," he returned carelessly, his gaze shifting to Sally to catch her reaction.

She looked embarrassed, pained by her mother's gloating. Her eyes flashed dismay at him before her lashes lowered, hiding her feelings. But they'd already been clear enough to Jack. She *cared* that he was apparently getting next to nothing from his father. A soft heart, not a greedy one. It made her even more appealing. And gave him another weapon to use in winning her over to what he wanted.

The muscles around his groin tightened.

He couldn't recall ever wanting a woman so much.

One way or another he was going to have Sally Maguire.

Every part of her.

Victor Newell cleared his throat with a come-to-attention cough and continued reading the will. "Contingent upon my wife, Ellen Mary Maguire surviving me by thirty days, I give her the remainder of my estate absolutely, and if she does not survive me by thirty days, I give the remainder of my estate in equal shares as tenants in common to my daughters, Sally Ann Maguire and Jane Therese Maguire."

He closed the folder and linked his hands across it, having completed the task of reading the legal document. A grimace of distaste preceded his next words. "I'm sorry to be the bearer of bad news, Lady Ellen, but I now have the onus of explaining to you that Sir Leonard's estate does not encompass a great deal."

The smug satisfaction on her face wavered. "What do you mean?" she asked sharply.

Jack focussed his attention on her. This was the pay line. This was why he'd stipulated that his father leave him a dollar, giving him the right to be here, to watch this woman get her comeuppance. She wouldn't be walking away with nothing, as his mother had, but her greedy heart was about to bleed. Not fatally. Just enough to balance the scales she had loaded against Jack all these years.

Victor Newell got straight to the point. "When Sir Leonard made this will a year ago, he was faced with bankruptcy and being charged with fraud."

"What?" The word exploded from Lady Ellen, shock followed by a gabble of disbelief. "He would have told me if he was in so much trouble."

"I'm sorry that he withheld this information from you," Victor said sympathetically. "Nevertheless, it is true. In building his transport empire, Sir Leonard was in the habit of skating close to the wind in regard to the law. He took risks, and eventually those risks caught up with him. He overextended with the airline, and everything was about to crash around him."

"But there was no hint of this," Lady Ellen argued vehemently, unable to accept what she was being told. "We kept living in the same manner."

"A matter of pride, I imagine. And I understand Sir Leonard always kept his home life separate from his business life. He was, in fact, facing a lengthy prison term on several counts, apart from losing everything. At this point in time, his son…" He nodded to Jack. "…offered him a rescue package."

A hiss of sharply indrawn breath from Lady Ellen.

Sally cocked her head, regarding Jack thoughtfully. She wasn't shocked. He sensed she was putting two and two together, weighing up what he'd done and why.

Jane's head was lowered, her eyes closed, her shoulders hunched over as though expecting a blow to fall. *Victim* slid into Jack's mind and he frowned over the word. There was something very wrong about Sally's younger sister. It wasn't just about what was happening today. A victim mentality was built up over years. By his father or Lady Ellen? Indifference could be an abuse in itself—his father's specialty—but Jack wouldn't put active cruelty past Lady Ellen.

He turned his gaze back to the woman he hated, watching her being hit by a savage reversal of fortune, wanting *her* to feel like a victim for once!

Victor was spelling out the details of the rescue package. "In effect, all the debts would be paid, the business empire would be maintained with the work force intact. Sir Leonard would hold the position of CEO with a salary of five million dollars a year. No one need know how the situation had been resolved. On the surface, everything could continue seamlessly."

"In return for what?" Lady Ellen snapped.

"A new will had to be written. *This* will." Victor tapped the manila folder. "Which stipulates that one dollar be granted to his son, with the rest of Sir Leonard's estate coming to you, Lady Ellen. However, that estate is very much diminished. Everything Mr. Jack Maguire had saved Sir Leonard from losing was legally signed over to him a year ago—every facet of the transport business, plus all personal assets, excluding only whatever Sir Leonard earned as CEO from the takeover onwards."

"*All* personal assets?" Lady Ellen wailed. "You can't mean our home."

"And its contents. Everything," the solicitor confirmed, then glanced appealingly at Jack. "You may be able to negotiate with Mr. Maguire about jewellery and other personal belongings."

Jack made no response. Let her stew, he thought, ruthlessly intent on giving her a taste of being shut out in the cold with nothing to hang on to. The look he gave her telegraphed, *You turned your back on me too many times, you mean-hearted bitch!*

"The horses," Sally said faintly, her face drained of colour.

They were important to her.

Jack filed that information away for future use.

"The horses were bought by Sir Leonard," Victor gently reminded her. "They were listed as his property. They now belong to his son. You must understand that all of these possessions would have been forcibly sold up, had Sir Leonard been declared bankrupt. You have continued to have the use of them, only because Mr.

Jack Maguire stepped in and allowed that to happen during his father's lifetime."

"It broke his heart!" Lady Ellen spat at Jack. "You killed him with your…your backstabbing takeover!"

Jack answered her heat with ice. "I believe a prison term and public disgrace would have broken his heart much earlier, Lady Ellen. My rescue package gave my father…gave all of you—" he shifted his gaze to Sally, wanting to hammer the truth home "—an extra year of the life you were accustomed to."

A life that had been closed to him when he was seven years old.

Sally was now twenty-four. She'd had the best of it up until now.

Her eyes said she knew it. There was sadness in them, but no hatred or blame for what he'd done. Did she feel the weight of justice on his side?

"And that year has provided you with an inheritance, Lady Ellen," Victor quickly pointed out. "Sir Leonard's investment broker has the details, but I believe it is in the vicinity of four million dollars."

"Four! But Leonard was worth billions!"

The burst of outrage confirmed her mercenary interests which, to Jack's mind, had always motivated her determination to keep him out of his father's life.

"Not at the end," Victor stated firmly.

"I'll fight this!" she declared vehemently, jumping to her feet, slamming her hands down on the table, leaning forward to fire her fury at the solicitor. "Possession is nine-tenths of the law. I'm going to keep my home. *He* made a mistake by letting us live in it." She turned a venomous glare to Jack. "Don't think for one minute you're going to take it from me."

"My father paid me rent for the Yarramalong property. You'll find you have no legal right to it," he advised her mockingly. "In fact, you'll be receiving an eviction notice when you return to it today."

"How dare you!" she fumed.

"Eviction for eviction, Lady Ellen." The words rolled sweetly off his tongue.

She puffed herself up with futile righteousness. "You won't get me out!"

Victor rose from his chair, picked up the manila folder and walked with great dignity to the end of the table. "I understand how deeply shocked you are, Lady Ellen," he said, presenting her with the folder. "However, I feel duty-bound to warn you that legally, the situation I have outlined to you is a *fait accompli*, and there are no grounds for contesting any part of it."

"We'll see about that," she snarled, snatching the folder from him and hurling a command at her daughters. "Girls, we're going!"

The two sisters instantly leapt to their feet, ready to obey.

"Sally!"

Her name whipped off Jack's tongue, cracking its own command for her attention.

Her head jerked towards him as he stood to

make his formidable presence felt. Her eyes held a kind of hopeless appeal, as though she wanted to give him the time he wanted but loyalty to her own family forbade it.

"I'd like to have a private word with you," he pressed.

"About what?" she asked quickly, almost breathlessly.

"You are not to speak to that man!" her mother sliced in, moving forward and grabbing Sally's arm to pull her away from any connection with him.

"The horses," Jack threw out.

It was enough to stop her from following her mother's lead. She resisted the tug of the maternal arm, glancing back at him in anxious inquiry.

"I wanted to discuss the future of the horses with you," Jack pushed, his eyes challenging her to make her own stand. "I know how committed you are to a career in showjumping."

He wasn't sure of that but it seemed likely bait for her to stay.

"Ignore him!" her mother insisted. "You can't trust a word he says. Come on."

"No." Boldly decisive. "I want to hear. I want to know."

"You're doing what *he* wants, you stupid girl."

"I'm not going to lose my horses if I don't have to."

Music to Jack's ears.

"You and Jane go on," Sally urged. "I'll catch up with you later."

"I wash my hands of you," her mother said furiously, releasing her arm and grabbing her sister's. "Come, Jane!"

They made a swift exit from the meeting room.

And Jack had what he'd aimed for…time alone with Sally Maguire…time to probe the inner workings of her mind and twist them to his advantage.

Just how far *would* she go in order to keep her horses and the lifestyle she had always enjoyed?

CHAPTER THREE

SALLY'S stomach was in knots. Her mother would tear her to shreds when she got home. But it wasn't their home anymore. It belonged to Jack Maguire. Everything did. And if she could save something from this total annihilation of all she'd known, why not give it a chance?

So what if he was intent on dishing out some humiliation! He'd taken it for years, being treated as an outcast from the family. She could take it, too. At least, she would find out what was on his mind, satisfy some of the interest he'd evoked in her.

"Would you like me to be present for this discussion?" the solicitor asked, jolting Sally into wheeling around to face Jack, her gaze whizzing to him for an answer.

"No, thank you, Victor. If I need to formalise an arrangement with Sally, I'll come back to you," he said smoothly, his handsome face showing nothing of his private thoughts. He smiled at her, charmingly persuasive, causing the knots in her stomach to develop flutters. "I thought we could ride up to the Skyroom Restaurant at the top of this building and chat informally over lunch. Is that agreeable to you?"

"Yes," she said. It seemed a very civilised arrangement to her. She didn't want this man to be an enemy, and hopefully, by spinning out lunch as long as possible, she could surely get a lot of information about him. Maybe even change his mind about the eviction order, or get it extended. Certainly being antagonistic was not going to win anything back from him. Perhaps nothing would, but at least this was a chance to try.

"Good!" A satisfied nod before addressing the solicitor again. "Thank you for your services this morning, Victor. Masterly, as always."

The solicitor harrumphed and waved them to the opened door where he still stood after seeing her mother and Jane out of the meeting room. Sally thanked him, too, as she passed him by, aware that his courtesy and diplomacy had not received any appreciation from her family. Shock didn't really excuse people behaving badly, she thought, wishing her mother had maintained some dignity instead of flying off the handle so aggressively. It didn't help the situation. It only reinforced Jack Maguire's inclination to be merciless.

He fell into step beside her in the corridor leading to the elevators, instantly making his presence felt. He didn't touch her, but the power of the man swept every other thought out of her mind, filling it with a whirl of speculation about what he might want with her. He couldn't really care about the horses. Nor could he really care about her. Yet…her whole body literally tingled with nervous anticipation.

They stepped into the elevator together. He pressed the button for the restaurant, then slanted a teasing little smile at her as the doors closed. "You don't always obey your mother's commands?"

"I'm not a little girl anymore," she said, her chin instinctively lifting in a tilt of self-determination.

"No, you're not," he agreed, a devilish appreciation of the fact twinkling from his vivid blue eyes.

Sally's breath caught in her throat. Was this luncheon invitation more about them—an exploration of an attraction that had nothing to do with the horses? He'd called her beautiful yesterday. But he couldn't have really meant it.

Her mother's warning rang in her ears... *You can't trust a word he says!*

Nevertheless, Sally's eyes were telling her he looked absolutely fabulous in his navy pinstripe suit, and every female hormone she had was buzzing with excitement at the possibility of a sexual connection with this man. However mad and bad of her it was to be even considering such a thing with Jack Maguire, she couldn't help what he made her feel, though a strong streak of self-respect demanded some caution about showing the impact he had on her.

"You said you lunched regularly with my father," she recalled, wondering if they'd dined in the Skyroom Restaurant together. "Did the two of you become close over the years?"

"Not in any father-and-son sense," came the dry reply, accompanied by a flash of irony. "He came to view me as a competitor in the business world and liked to keep tabs on what I was doing."

"You must have kept tabs on what he was doing, as well," Sally remarked, pointedly adding, "for you to step in and offer a rescue package."

"Yes." It was a matter-of-fact reply, no elaboration offered.

"He must have been grateful to you," Sally prodded.

His laugh was derisive. So were his eyes. "He hated it. Quite simply, the alternative to not taking my offer was worse."

"Why did you do it?" It was the most pertinent question, going directly to the heart of the man.

"Oh, there was a certain piquancy about getting by force what was denied me in any natural way," he drawled, watching her reaction with glittering interest.

To Sally, it was sad that he had never been able to achieve the natural relationship he had sought with his father. Lost years when he was in America, years of trying after he'd returned to Australia, the continual sense of rejection.... "I'm sorry you didn't get what you wanted, Jack," she said softly.

His face tightened. His eyes narrowed to sizzling slits. He didn't like her sympathy, didn't want it. Sally tensed, expecting some kind of hit back at her, but the moment of venom passed and mockery took its place.

"But I did, Sally. With the bonus of taking from your mother the hallowed home which I was never allowed to darken."

The little hope in her heart died. There would be no softening over the eviction.

"Would you have darkened it if the welcome

mat had been put out for you?" she asked, remembering the day he had been turned away.

He shrugged. "If I had ever been welcomed in
my father's home, many things might have been
different. As it is…people reap what they sow."
His lips twitched in sardonic amusement. "And
I make a very good Grim Reaper."

Dark and diabolical.

A little shiver ran down Sally's spine.

Was her mother right? Should she leave now,
not listen to any deal he might put to her? Was
she playing into his hands—hands that couldn't
be trusted—by staying with him?

The elevator came to a halt.

The doors slid open.

He gestured for her to precede him out of the
compartment.

Her gaze flicked up to his, fearful, uncertain.
The biting blue eyes glittered with challenge,
calling her a coward if she failed to respond. Her
feet moved forward even while her heart
hammered at the thought she was walking

straight into a lion's den. But they would be surrounded by other people while they had lunch. It wasn't as though they'd be really alone, she told herself, so what harm could come to her?

She let him escort her into the restaurant and pretended to be captivated by its spectacular view over Sydney as they were led to a table for two and seated comfortably in plush armchairs upholstered in blue. It truly was a sky room. Even the blue and white décor was designed to make the occupants feel they were floating on clouds, looking down on the world. A waiter handed them luncheon menus and took an order of two glasses of champagne from Jack before leaving them to decide on what they wanted to eat.

She looked at him then—the man who now owned everything her father had built—her eyes deriding his choice of drink. "Do you expect me to toast your victory, Jack?"

He laughed, amused by her defiance. It lightened his face, making him look wickedly attractive, causing Sally's pulse to skitter into a wild beat. She took a deep breath in an attempt to calm herself and he seemed amused by that, too, enjoying the power he was exerting over her.

"I'm in the mood to celebrate," he drawled.

"The king is dead. Long live the king?" she shot back at him, bridling against any levity over her father's death.

He shook his head, his expression sobering. "Did you love him, Sally?"

She hesitated, realising she had not really been grieving over her father's death, the initial shock of it gradually giving way to apprehension about what it would mean to her own and Jane's lives. Sir Leonard Maguire had been more like a dominating presence, someone who demanded his due for what he gave, rather than a father who naturally inspired a caring closeness. His coldness towards Jane had not endeared him to Sally.

"He was not an easy man to love," she said truthfully. "But there were some good times with him."

"Did he love you?"

Again she was thrown into examining her relationship with the man who had denied Jack any love, which made her acutely aware of the wound she might give if she answered yes. Though she didn't think that was the truth anyway.

"He was not the kind of man to show open affection," she answered slowly. "But I know he liked me and was proud of my achievements in showjumping."

"You performed for him," Jack commented sardonically.

Pride made her say, "I performed more for myself."

He nodded. "Earning his approval."

She couldn't deny it. The best times with her father had been when she'd won. If she made mistakes, rode badly, disappointed him…he turned away from her as though she didn't belong to him. Which always hurt no matter how much she mentally armoured herself against it, silently vowing she'd do better next time.

"What about Jane?"

Too many hurts there. Despite all her younger

sister's efforts to please their father, Sally had always felt Jane, at best, was only ever tolerated by him, but she wasn't about to say so, to lay out Jane's problems to a man who had every reason not to care about them, might even find some satisfaction in the misery of one of the adopted daughters.

"We're not here to talk about my sister," she reminded him.

He shrugged. "Just curious. My mother said he had no love in him. Which was certainly my experience. I wondered if it was true for you and Jane."

It gave her pause for thought. Was he simply trying to make sense of what had happened between him and their father? It was difficult to make comparisons. Sir Leonard *had* expected them to perform for him, all in their separate ways. He had provided them with everything and they had shown their appreciation by keeping his home life as pleasant as they could. It was what their mother had trained them to do.

He had been the lynch pin around which their lives had revolved. Now that he was gone, they were adrift.

She hadn't ever *loved* her father. What had always been instilled in her was a respect for who he was—the rich powerful man who had given her the chance to do what she wanted and applauded her for it. She didn't love her mother, either, having picked up from early childhood that "dutiful daughter" was the role she was required to fulfil, never a needy one wanting too much time and attention. She and Jane had been well and truly taught their place in the Maguire household.

But what was their place now?

The sense of loss crashed down on her again.

Would Jack Maguire offer some kind of life raft for her to cling to?

"Is there any love in you?" she asked, searching his face for a soft answer.

There was none. "I loved my mother. She died when I was twenty," he stated grimly.

Before he returned to Australia and ran straight into the stonewall rejection of both his father and stepmother. A life emptied of any family, she thought, his natural place taken by her and Jane. Did he hate them for it?

"Do you love Lady Ellen, Sally?"

She sighed, a heavy weight dragging on her heart. "What was done to you was wrong—shutting you out of our lives—but you wouldn't have fitted into my mother's regime, Jack."

"She was the queen and you had to pay homage to her?"

She winced at the description but was unable to deny how apt it was. "There were rules made. Rules that had to be kept for the sake of harmony in the home."

"And now? When there is no home?" he pushed, leaning forward, keenly interested in her reply.

She managed an ironic smile. "The whole basis for those rules no longer exists. We face chaos."

He returned the ironic smile as he relaxed back in his chair. "Not necessarily. Not you, Sally."

His eyes simmered with the promise of other possibilities. The singling out of herself made her feel uneasy. "What do you mean…not me?"

The waiter interrupted, serving them with glasses of champagne, asking for their luncheon choices. Sally glanced distractedly at the menu and picked out the fish dish, thinking it would be the easiest to eat. Jack casually ordered the same, plus a platter of hors d'oeuvres for starters. The waiter departed and Sally stared at Jack, waiting to be enlightened. He picked up his glass of champagne in a teasing toast.

"Let's drink to a harmonious settlement between us."

"Like what?" she demanded, tentatively reaching for her glass, hoping he would offer something acceptable.

His eyes weighed up her eagerness. "What do you want me to offer you, Sally?" he asked.

"You said we'd talk about the horses," she swiftly reminded him.

"You love your horses."

"Yes, I do."

He cocked a challenging eyebrow. "More than you love Lady Ellen?"

She frowned, not wanting to make any comparison.

"You've already taken one step away from her in your desire to keep what you've had," he pointed out. "I'm wondering how many steps you're prepared to take." His mouth formed a very sensual moue. "Will you throw in your lot with me or will you run home to Mummy?"

Sally bridled at the thought of running home to Mummy. Her parting remark "I wash my hands of you" typified her mother's tyrannical attitude: Do what I say or suffer the consequences. Becoming her whipping boy for the loss of what she had believed would be her inheritance did not appeal, and Sally had no doubt that would be her role. And Jane's. If they remained dependent on her mother for anything.

"I have my own life to live," she said, determined on finding a way to do it. "That's a third choice, Jack, which doesn't involve either you or my mother."

"A brave choice…starting from nothing," he remarked, his eyes sceptical of her ability to make good on her own.

"How did you start?" she threw back at him, wanting to know how he'd come to be so wealthy.

He ignored the question, boring in on her. "You're twenty-four years old, Sally, with no training for anything apart from a sport which requires a great deal of financial backing. What do you see yourself doing with your life?"

"Did *you* have financial backing?" she persisted, having had too little time to think about her own situation to make a list of employment possibilities.

"A stable hand?" he mocked, still boring in on her. "Looking after other people's horses?"

"I could be hired to ride them. That's done in showjumping competition," she said belligerently.

"Second-string horses? At the whim of another owner? Whom you might disappoint?" He shook his head. "Not what you're used to, Sally."

She flushed at the reminder of how easy it had been for her, while he... "How did you start?" she repeated insistently.

He shrugged. "I found I had a talent for poker. I won millions of dollars at poker tournaments around the world. When I'd built up a big enough stake, I diversified, finding investments that turned a quick profit. It's all about playing the percentages."

His eyes targeted hers with riveting intensity. "Throwing your lot in with me is a much higher percentage play for you than trying to find work at the bottom of the pile."

It felt as though a jackhammer was attacking her heart. Jack Maguire was intent on making her choose to do what he wanted. She suddenly knew that with absolute certainty. Whether it would be another triumph for him to draw her away from her family and plant her at his side, or whether he was simply acting on an attraction he wanted to satisfy, she didn't know. Maybe both.

"You haven't told me what throwing my lot in with you entails," she said, trying her utmost to look as though she was objectively weighing up the situation and not helplessly affected by a hormonal rush of excitement.

His mouth curved into a quirky little smile. "Sir Leonard's secretary told me that when my father flew home each evening, Lady Ellen always met him at the property's helipad, beautifully dressed for dinner and with a martini in hand ready to pass it to him. Is that true?"

"Yes."

"She devotedly serviced all his needs."

The sexual glitter in his eyes played havoc with her nerves.

"I don't know what went on in their bedroom," she blurted out.

"Oh, I have no doubt Sir Leonard got whatever he wanted. That was Lady Ellen's power. Why would a man give up being king of his castle for a son who couldn't give him what his wife did? My father played the percentages, too."

Love didn't come into it, she thought. Love wouldn't come into any proposition Jack Maguire laid out, either. The butterflies in her stomach folded their wings, leaving it feeling strangely hollow. Yet the sense that her future was bound up with this man did not go away.

The waiter returned, set a platter of hors d'oeuvres on the table between them, checked that their glasses of champagne didn't need refilling, and left them alone again.

"The situation is this, Sally," Jack said, leaning forward to pick up a smoked salmon roll and move it to the side of the plate. "That represents your horses." Egg and caviar on a little circle of toast was similarly shifted. "The facilities you use—stables, horse truck, training field." A quiche tartlet followed. "Financial support, vet fees, showjumping competition fees, all operational costs." Sun-dried tomato on mozzarella. "Sole mistress of the house you have always called home, overseeing its running and the running of the property, with the same staff if they want to stay, hiring others if they want to leave. A generous salary for you to maintain the status quo…"

He went on and on, moving the hors d'ouevres to one side in a slow, mesmerising fashion, listing the privileges she had enjoyed and adding the responsibilities which had previously been her mother's. When there was only one small delicacy left untouched, he lifted his gaze to hers, intent on pushing the decision he wanted.

"You can have the loaded side of the plate—" He pointed to the lone, untouched crab tartlet "—or you can go with Lady Ellen. One or the other, Sally."

No bending on that point. She could feel his ruthless drive to cut her mother out, to cut her to the quick by replacing her with one of the daughters she'd adopted to replace him in his father's life.

Sally stared down at the almost empty side of the plate, knowing if she took his deal, she would probably never see her mother again, forever branded as an ungrateful traitor. She was probably that already by agreeing to this lunch with him.

Her gaze shifted to the life he was offering... so tempting. But could he be trusted to deliver on his word if she took his deal? What if he only meant to create as much disharmony in her family as he could and she was being suckered into playing a role in his vengeful game?

She gestured to the loaded side, her eyes searching his for some indication of his motivation. "What do you get out of this, Jack?"

He leaned back in his chair, regarding her with a whimsical look that seemed to be mocking himself for whatever was driving him. The expression in his eyes slowly changed, gathering a hypnotic intensity. She felt the force of the man being channelled straight into her, reaching for her heart, her mind, her soul, determined on bending her to his will. Then he spoke the words she had secretly wanted to hear.

"I get you, Sally."

CHAPTER FOUR

JACK felt the charge of adrenaline that invariably accompanied risking his hand in a high-
stakes poker game. Would she go all in or
would she fold?

A tide of heat washed up her lovely long neck.
Her cheeks bloomed with colour, making the
green of her eyes more pronounced—eyes that
had unmistakably telegraphed interest in him.
Jack knew he was an attractive package to
women, especially with wealth heightening his
sex appeal. She shouldn't baulk at having him
added to the deal, not with so much else being
offered, but at only twenty-four, she might still
be young enough to be nursing romantic ideals.

Love and marriage were not on the table.

He had no intention of holding them out to her.

She took a deep breath. Her eyes didn't waver from his. There was no pretending she didn't know what he meant in them. She was taking it in, sifting through what it would mean to her. He found himself surprisingly tense as he waited for her reply, willing her to give in to him. In the end she didn't answer him, choosing to do a bit of probing herself.

"Why me?"

Not "no." Not "yes," either. It was an astute question, delving into his motivation. He'd never paid for sex in his life, not in such an upfront fashion as this. Occasionally gifts afterwards, in appreciation of pleasure given. So why was he prepared to lay out so much for Sally Maguire?

Because she wouldn't come to the man who'd stripped her of everything.

He had to give back in order to make it possible, and what it cost didn't matter to him.

But she could take the view he was setting her

up as his whore. Her pride might get in the way if he left the deal too cut-and-dried. Better to colour it with feelings she could empathise with. Women related to emotion and Sally had shown considerable sensitivity to the injustice to him in their family situation.

"I believe you would have welcomed me home," he said softly. "I think you've been very conscious of the fact that I was not allowed any place at the Yarramalong property and didn't think it was right. Is that so, Sally?"

She nodded.

"You alone," he emphasised.

"I don't think Jane would have minded," she said quickly.

Jane—she cared very much about her sister—a victim in the Maguire household. Jack was certain of it now, given the pained look on Sally's face when he'd asked if Jane had been loved. She would want to save her more fragile sister from any further abuse from Lady Ellen. Oddly enough, he did, too. No one should remain a victim of that woman. If he gave Sally more than enough money to cover both sisters' needs, it should achieve two purposes—Jane's freedom and Sally's compliance with his plan.

"Jane would not be here with me, as you are," he pointed out.

She knew it as well as he did. The younger adopted daughter had scuttled after her mother like a frightened mouse. Before Sally could say any more in defence of her sister, he went on describing what he hoped was a seductive vision.

"It's you I feel a connection with, Sally. I remember watching you jumping your horse all those years ago. Poetry in motion. I like the idea of your being there, keeping everything up as it was. Only, this time it would be there for me, too. Not that I intend to live at the property with you, but I'd like to visit from time to time, feel the sense of homecoming that my father always enjoyed." He constructed a whimsical little smile. "Being welcomed with a smile and a martini. Going riding with you. Enjoying your company. That sounds very good to me."

"You ride?"

It wasn't so much probing for more information this time but a spark of pleasure in the idea that they could share something other than a bedroom. Which they could. He *would* enjoy riding with her.

"Much of my youth was spent on a horse. I worked on my stepfather's ranch before and after school. I could certainly help you exercise your horses," he offered with a smile.

She smiled back.

It was an instinctive response, almost immediately quashed.

She wasn't won yet, but Jack knew he was making ground with her. Besides, if the idea of being available for occasional sex with him had been totally unpalatable, she would have slapped him down with a definite no by now. The weird part was he found the vision he'd laid out for her very seductive himself. Having places to live—even palatial penthouse apart-ments—had always been nothing more than conveniences for him. Could Sally Maguire give him a sense of coming home? It would be inter-esting to find out.

The waiter reappeared, gesturing to the uneaten hors d'oeuvres. "Is there something wrong, sir?"

Jack wickedly waved to the loaded side of the plate. "Would you like to sample one, Sally?"

She shook her head.

Not ready to commit herself yet, Jack thought. He was tempted to eat the one representing her monster mother, but decided that might be too in-her-face offensive. "Take it away," he in-structed the waiter. "We'll enjoy the main course when it comes."

The waiter removed the plate and himself.

Silence from Sally, her beautiful eyes downcast, hands in her lap, sitting very straight, closed in upon herself…thinking what?

Jack tossed up whether he should push or be

patient. He needed to know how her mind was working so he could counter any negatives and drive forward on the positives. Silence gave him nothing.

"Do we have a deal, Sally?" he asked quietly, forcing her to acknowledge his presence.

The veiling lashes slowly lifted. Bright green eyes looked directly at him, sharply intelligent eyes that demanded no evasion. "Do you see me as family—a sister you'd like to have—or are you intent on having me as your kept woman on the side, for as long as I give you satisfaction?"

Heat raced into her cheeks again as she bluntly voiced the second option. Her chin tilted defiantly. She was determined on getting the unvarnished truth from him, regardless of how much heartburn it gave her.

She was gut-wrenchingly beautiful.

And she was skewering him with those eyes.

The sense of walking a tightrope to get to the end he wanted was very strong. "Hardly a kept woman when you will be earning your keep," he answered. "And I have no doubt you will run the property to my satisfaction. Would a manager's salary of a hundred thousand dollars a year be acceptable?"

He didn't care if it took him the whole year to get Sally Maguire, have her he would.

"A hundred thousand?" she repeated incredulously.

It had to be more than enough to set Jane up independently, as well as looking after Sally's personal needs. He'd already promised to take care of all other expenses. Right now it probably sounded suspiciously too much, but give her enough time to think about what she could do with that money...

"It's a very valuable property," he reminded her. "Worth millions. I want it to hold its value. I'm sure you'll do your best to maintain it as it should be maintained. I trust you to do that. And to ensure you can trust me to deliver on my word, we can go back to Victor Newell after lunch and have him draw up a legal contract between us."

"For a year," she murmured, weighing it up in her mind.

"To begin with." He might want her longer than that. Already the excitement of the chase was firing up his blood. He suspected if he spun out the time with her, she could keep him very enticingly engaged. More so than any other woman he'd known.

Her eyes refocused on his. The distraction of the tempting contract was clearly set aside. 'You didn't answer my first question, Jack.'

Straight back to the sexual angle!

The devil in him prompted a provocative question. "Would you like me to treat you as my sister, Sally?"

"I'm not," she replied so quickly, so emphatically, he almost laughed with a heady sense of triumph. The woman in her was definitely responding to the man in him.

He brought the burst of exhilaration under control and gave her some rope to hang on to. "That's not my view of you, either. However, let me assure you I've never bought sex from a woman. As I said, I would like to be welcomed by you whenever I visit the property, but…" He shrugged. "Is that too much to ask of you?"

She frowned. "No. As my employer, you'd be entitled to a ready welcome."

So sleeping with the boss was okay?

It was what her mother had done.

Was Sally Maguire of the same ilk?

Time would tell.

All he needed from her at this point was a yes to the contract, which would give him the open door to pursuing her at his leisure. He leaned forward, bringing all the force of his personality into play.

"Seize the day, Sally!"

Seize the day.…

Sally wanted to. It was a plum job. A hundred thousand dollars a year, with all expenses paid, being able to carry on what she loved doing. And with that amount of money at her disposal, she could support Jane through her last two semesters at university, pay her part of the rent on the apartment she shared with other students, give her an allowance, set it up so she was completely independent of their mother and her demands. It would give her sister the chance of making a life of her own, free of the rants and raves over the knock of fortune that would inevitably make their mother mean.

Sally had no illusions on that score. However, she did feel confused about what Jack wanted from her. Was it the home he'd never had? He wouldn't pay so much for sex with her, would he? He was so attractive, he could have plenty of women for nothing—truly beautiful women, like those she'd seen photographed with him at high-society events.

Were those devilish blue eyes really twinkling with sexy excitement at the prospect of her getting into bed with him, or did he give any passably attractive woman that look as a matter of course? Passably attractive was all she could be to him.

Carrots they'd called her at school because of her wretchedly unruly red curls sticking out everywhere. And she hated having the pasty white skin that always needed multi applications of blockout cream to prevent burning or, horror of horrors to her mother, freckling. She was more an oddity than a beauty. Yesterday she'd been sure he'd only called her beautiful at the funeral to spite her mother, and that was definitely the more likely truth.

She was the one wanting him, not the other way around. It was embarrassing to think now of how she had questioned him so directly on being his *kept woman.* Having what his father had known—the home he'd denied Jack—had to be driving his offer. It couldn't be wanting a whole year of sex with her. That made no sense. Besides, he'd just assured her that sex was not a given in the deal, hadn't he?

A year would give her time to look around for other opportunities she might take up in the future, should this deal with Jack Maguire turn sour. Right now she simply didn't know the heart of the man. Only time would tell her if the *connection* she felt between them could develop into the kind of relationship she'd love to have with him. A year would be long enough to find out.

"Okay. I'll take that contract," she said decisively, her eyes challenging his integrity on every word of it.

He grinned, his delight in her acceptance making her heart dance in a wild hip-hop. "I'll set it up right now," he said, whipping a small silver cell phone from his suit pocket.

He spoke to Victor Newell's secretary, dictating the terms he had outlined to Sally and asking for the contract to be drawn up and ready for their signatures by the time they'd finished lunch. He cocked a challenging eyebrow at her as he put the 'phone away. "Satisfied?"

Her mouth had gone dry, drained of moisture by a last-minute attack of nerves. "Yes," she croaked, acutely aware that she was not only signing a year of her life to him, but quite possibly making a permanent break from the woman who had adopted and raised her.

An ungrateful daughter.

A serpent daughter, dancing with the devil.

But hadn't her mother brought this situation upon herself by being so set against Jack? If she'd accepted him as a stepson, let him into their lives…

"So let's now drink to something good coming out of this," Jack purred at her, lifting his glass of champagne in a toast.

She snatched up her own glass and clinked it with his. "Something good," she repeated with reckless fervour, and drank, wanting the bubbles to go straight to her brain and blow out all the worries about taking a wrong jump and rushing headlong into bad territory.

CHAPTER FIVE

LUNCH over, contract signed, Jack accompanied Sally down to street level and offered her a limousine ride home.

She quickly declined, preferring to make her own way rather than arrive in grand style, looking as though she was revelling in her defection to the man who was taking over everything. Including her. More or less.

"Thank you for the lunch and the contract," she said, offering her hand in a businesslike fashion.

His eyes simmered with sexy amusement as he wrapped his fingers around hers. "Call me if you have any problems you can't resolve yourself," he said with a quirky little smile.

Up until that moment he hadn't touched her.

The warmth and strength of his hand, the confidence in his eyes, the whole aura of a master of manipulation at work, made Sally acutely aware of how vulnerable she was to this man's power.

"You put me in charge. I'll be in charge," she asserted, not wanting to appear weak in any way whatsoever. "When can I expect you to visit?"

The smile broadened into a grin that reawakened the butterflies in her stomach. "I'll let you know."

"I'll need fair warning if you want me to put out the welcome mat."

"Of course," he agreed. "I shall enjoy the thrill of anticipation."

Her heart started leaping all over the place. *Don't think about it. Just get on with it,* her mind frantically dictated. "Well, I'll see you when I see you," she almost gabbled. "Goodbye for now, Jack."

She quickly withdrew her hand and spun away from him, walking blindly down Martin Place to Wynyard Station, guiltily conscious of the thrill of anticipation playing merry hell with her female hormones.

A train to Wyong.

Call home to get someone to pick me up.

Work out how to face my mother and Jane with all this.

Her mind kept reiterating what it had to concentrate on, trying to overcome the wild dance of nervous excitement Jack Maguire had set in motion. She had to deal with him in the future. Somehow. But right now she had very immediate concerns that needed her full attention.

It took her most of the two-hour train journey to sober up completely and get her head around how best to present the deal to her mother. On a purely common-sense basis, it meant one daughter would not be a financial drain on her. Neither would the other if Jane agreed to Sally's plan. The big problem was…would her mother be in the mood to listen? And was she going to accept eviction?

Sally suspected a major tantrum was going on at home. When she'd called to request a pick-up from the station, Jeanette Deering, the house-keeper, had sounded badly distracted, hemming and hawing anxiously before deciding her husband, Graham, could meet the train—Graham, who was supposed to maintain security at the property, keeping out trespassers. Like Jack Maguire. Did they already know Jack couldn't be kept out anymore?

When she walked out of the station at Wyong, Graham had his Land Rover handily parked and his big frame was propped against the driver's door, beefy arms folded, a grim look on his darkly weathered face. He and Jeanette had been in her father's employ at the Yarramalong property all Sally's life and she was fond of both of them. Never before had Graham greeted her without a smile.

"A bad day. A bad, bad day," he muttered as he rounded the vehicle to open the passenger door for her. "Don't know what we're all going to do now, Sally."

"Mum told you about the takeover?"

"Didn't have to. There's a security van parked at the gate. Some legal bloke served an eviction notice." He shook his head. "Seems like there's no fighting it. And Lady Ellen sure isn't taking kindly to having her home taken from her."

Which was probably a huge understatement, Sally thought, her chest tightening at the prospect of delivering her news. At least it would be good for the staff on the property, she assured herself, giving them another year to sort out their lives. She waited until they were on the road to Yarramalong before saying, "You can stay on at the property if you want to, Graham. You and Jeanette and the rest of the staff."

"No." He sighed dolefully. "Have to look for another position, Sally. Lady Ellen told us she can't afford to pay our salaries anymore."

Sally took a deep breath and baldly announced, "Jack Maguire will pay them. He's already set up the money for that to be done. Pay me, too, for staying on and managing the property. He wants to keep everything as it is, so you don't have to go."

He threw her a startled look. "But Lady Ellen said…"

"I've signed a contract with him," Sally stated firmly. "I assure you what I'm saying is true. He'll keep you on. Only my mother has to go."

He sucked in a long breath, returned his attention to the road, then muttered, "Lady Ellen won't like it."

"I can't help that. It isn't negotiable. Eviction for eviction," Sally explained, repeating Jack's words.

"I was the one who turned him away all those years ago," Graham said worriedly.

"On my mother's orders. I'm sure he doesn't blame you for it."

Silence while he chewed over the situation. "Jack Maguire…he's not going to live here?"

"No. He'll visit from time to time. That's all."

"And you stay on."

"Yes. The contract is for a year."

"A year…" More cogitating, then, "I reckon Jeanette and I will stay on for a while. See how it goes."

Sally sighed in relief. "That would be a big help to me. Will you inform the rest of the staff what the new arrangement is, Graham? I think I'm going to have my hands full, telling my mother and dealing with the fallout."

"I don't envy you that job," he said with feeling. "Lady Ellen sure doesn't like things not going her way." He shot her a concerned look. "Want me to stand by?"

She shook her head. This was something she had to do herself. It was too personal to involve anyone else. "Thank you, but I think I can weather the storm."

"It's bad," he warned. "I'll be in the kitchen with Jeanette if you need some support. And don't worry about the staff. I'll let everyone know what's going on."

"Thanks, Graham. I'd appreciate all the support I can get in the weeks ahead while I find my feet as the resident manager."

"Don't see any problem there. I reckon the staff will feel so grateful to be kept on, they'll work their butts off for you. You'll see. Jack Maguire won't find anything to criticise when he comes to visit. Place will be picture-perfect. As always."

Picture-perfect...

It was...the most beautiful property in the valley...evoking a poignant swell of emotion in Sally as it came into view. The lush green fields, the white fences, the artfully placed clusters of shade trees for the horses, the architect designed stables and barn, the beautiful avenue of maples leading up to the big white house on the hill...this had been the only home she'd known, and the sense of loss that seized her heart also brought a blur of tears to her eyes.

Her father gone.

The home he'd given them gone.

She hadn't saved anything. The contract with Jack simply put the loss of this property and all that went with it on hold for a year. Still, it did give everyone time to come to terms with change and that was good, wasn't it?

Everyone except her mother. Whose loss was
much greater since she had expected a billion-
dollar inheritance. Sally told herself there was
nothing she could do about that. She'd try to be
as sympathetic as her mother allowed her to be,
but a bad storm probably meant abuse flying
everywhere.

A security van was parked at the gate. A man
got out of it, identified Graham and waved him
on. It was a sober reminder that Jack Maguire
did not trust her mother and was ensuring that
nothing went into or out of the property without
being checked. He was clearly determined on
having all he'd paid for.

Did that mean her, too?

Sex wasn't in the deal, she forcefully
reminded herself. Though barely fifteen minutes
later, to Sally's churning horror, her mother was
not only making that assumption but throwing
out a string of shocking advice on how to make
capital out of it.

Jeanette had met her at the front door and

directed her into the main lounge room where several valuable vases had been smashed on the parquet floor. Her mother had been pacing back and forth in front of the great sandstone fireplace, downing a scotch on the rocks while haranguing Jane, who was cowered in the corner of one of the three matching leather chesterfields. The tirade had been instantly re-aimed at Sally, a disloyal bitch for kowtowing to her father's killer. Then had come the derisive demand to know what she'd got out of it.

Sally had moved in to stand beside where her sister sat, laying a comforting hand on Jane's stiffly hunched shoulder, then, in as calm a voice as she could muster, laid out the terms of the contract she had signed, expecting another burst of outrage at her perfidy in taking on what should remain in her mother's hands. Yet her announcement had not provoked more fury. Her mother had gone completely still, her eyes narrowing to thoughtful slits, her mouth slowly thinning into a smug little smile.

"You've got him!" she'd said maliciously, then broke into a peal of laughter that was somehow more chilling than any vicious words she might have spoken.

"Men!" she'd crowed. "No matter how clever they are, the brain below their belts is their weak point. Jack Maguire gave himself away at the funeral service yesterday, saying you were beautiful. He's using this contract to set you up as his mistress, his grateful little mistress who'll do anything he wants to keep her horses. The trick is to do precisely that—give him whatever sex he likes, make it so good he'll keep coming back, ensuring you have enough time with him to get yourself pregnant. Have his child and you can take him for a damned good slice of *his* billions! Tit for tat!"

Sally could only stare at her mother, totally rocked by this view of what she should do. Having sex for money was heart-shrivelling enough. Everything within her recoiled at the idea of deliberately setting out to have a baby for money. A baby should be wanted by both parents, loved by both parents. She was here in this moment because she hadn't been wanted or loved enough, handed over to an adoption agency, abandoned by her natural parents. Never would she have a child for financial profit! Never!

It was Jane who voiced shocked protest. "You can't mean for Sally to have a child without… without the security of marriage!"

"Having Jack Maguire's child will give her all the security she's ever going to need," was whipped back at her. "Use your head, Jane. You'll never be poor if your sister's rich."

"But having a baby just to…"

"Oh, for pity's sake! Why do you think I worked at getting you two adopted?" came the scathing demand.

"Because…because you couldn't have children of your own?" Jane answered weakly, sounding unsure and confused.

"That was what I told Leonard." The words were laced with utter contempt for his belief in her act of deceit. "The truth was I didn't want to spoil my figure with a pregnancy. Having a great body and giving him great sex was how I'd got Leonard to shed his first wife and marry me. I wasn't about to let some other cow take him from me the same way, but you never know with men. So I needed to tie him up with children, ensure that if he ever thought of dumping me it would cost him big-time. And to find now, it's all been for nothing..." She gnashed her teeth in disgust.

"Hardly nothing. You do get four million dollars," Sally reminded her, feeling a huge tide of disgust herself. All these years...she and Jane had been nothing but an insurance policy to the woman who had adopted them. Not daughters. Just assets to be cashed in if her marriage didn't last the distance. No doubt they were now lia-bilities to be shed.

"Peanuts!" Her eyes glowered a warning at

both of them. "And I'll need every cent of it to set me up and look attractive to another man of means."

No grown-up daughters in that scene! And no financial support would be forthcoming for either of them. "I imagine a fashionable apartment in Sydney would be a first step," Sally put forward, testing for a fuller picture.

"Yes," her mother snapped, chin lifting in scornful pride. "I wouldn't have stayed on this country property anyway, now that Leonard's gone. But I can pretend it's still mine with you here, Sally. Jack Maguire has played right into our hands. And when you have him by the balls, you can remunerate me for all I've given you over the years."

My father gave it, not you, Sally thought. You only ever put on a show of mothering us in front of him. And that's gone. An overwhelming sense of emptiness made her voice completely flat as she said, "I'm not like you. I'll never be like you. I have no intention of getting Jack

Maguire by the balls. I'm just going to fulfil my contract with him."

"Don't be such a naïve fool! You've got an open door opportunity to secure everything you've had up until now. More!"

Sally shook her head. "I won't do it that way. I won't deceive him and I won't play your game of deception, either. This place is his, fair and square, and I'm glad to have a job because I know I can't expect any support from you, Mother. Jane and I have served your purpose. We've been your mannequins in a show to keep our father tied to you, but that's over. We are now expendable, aren't we?"

"Sally, what are you saying?" Jane cried, frightened of where this was leading.

Sally squeezed her shoulder in quick reassurance. "Don't worry. You'll always have me."

"You ungrateful little sod!" her mother screeched. "You were nothing before I gave you a home. You've had every privilege any girl could want. Both of you! And what do I get in return?"

Sally refused to be shamed into backing down. "We played your game. That's what you got in return," she shot back at her mother, hating the sense of having been acquired as a weapon in the war for wealth. She could have been adopted by someone else, someone who would have really loved her—loved Jane.

"If you had any sense you'd be still playing it," her mother jeered.

Sally answered with steely pride. "I won't be your pawn anymore."

"You stupid, stupid girl! Don't you realise my advice could turn you into a queen?"

"It's not what I want."

That was the truth of it. She wanted to love the man she had a baby with, wanted him to love her back, both of them loving parents to their child. All the money in the world couldn't buy that.

"You want to spend your life mucking out stables?" her mother demanded in towering scorn.

"At least it's honest muck. It doesn't hurt anybody," Sally flashed back at her.

She snorted. "Don't tell me Leonard got hurt by what I did. Nor you and Jane, living in the lap of luxury."

It has hurt Jane, Sally thought grimly, knowing her sister had never felt emotionally secure in this home. Not me so much because I had the horses to escape to. But most of all... "It hurt Jack," she said, knowing that was irrefutable—a little boy robbed of his father, replaced by two girls born to other people.

"Dear Jack." Venom dripped off her mother's tongue. "He hurt so bad he became a billionaire. You expect me to feel sorry for him?" Her eyes glittered with malice. "You mark my words. You've walked into his trap, signing this contract, and he'll take you down. The only way to beat that is to take him down first."

"I guess that's what you did all those years ago, Mother. Do you think taking him down served your best interests in the long run?" Sally challenged. "Seems to me he beat you in the end."

Her face twisted with rage. "We'll come out on top if you do what I say."

"I won't do it," Sally threw back at her determinedly.

Her mother charged across the room in a fury, arm swinging out to hit. Sally barely had time to twist aside and raise her own arm to block the blow before it struck.

"Run to the kitchen and get Graham, Jane," she yelled at her sister. Then to her mother who was completely out of control, attacking with frightening persistence. "You'd better stop this right now because we're not going to take any more abuse from you." Her sister was still scrunched up like a mesmerised bunny. "Jane, go!"

She finally snapped into action, scrambling off the chesterfield and pelting out of the room.

"You want to be charged with assault, Mother? I'll do it. I promise you I'll do it," Sally asserted fiercely, frantically fending off more blows. "Graham will come and do what I say because Jack Maguire employs him now. Under my management. I'm the boss, not you. How will it look to your wealthy friends if you get charged with assaulting your daughter?"

That got through to her.

She lowered her arms to her sides, hands clenched into tight fists, her chest heaving with frustration, her eyes wild with killing fervour. "Some daughter you are!" she spat.

The dutiful daughter had died in this room. It was one more grief adding pain to the load in Sally's heart. "You never really made me feel you were my mother," she said sadly.

It evoked a vicious reply. "I hope one of your damned horses throws you and tramples you to death."

The last thread of any sense of loyalty broke. There was no room left for smoothing over this ruction. Sally steeled herself to draw a final line under it. "I suggest you pack up and go to wherever you feel good about yourself, because staying here is not going to work for you."

Graham charged into the room, Jane hovering

nervously behind him. "You need some help, Sally?" he asked, looking belligerently at his former employer.

Sally grimly made the call. "I think we're finished here, aren't we, Mother?"

Not without one last sting. "Your father would turn in his grave if he knew how you were treating me."

Sally stared her down, denying her the satisfaction of seeing any evidence of a guilt trip. Besides which, she felt no guilt. None at all. She and Jane had done their best to please their father while he was alive. That need to please had ended with his death.

Lady Ellen puffed herself up and started to stalk out of the room in high dudgeon. She snapped her fingers at Jane. "You can come and help me pack."

"No. Jane stays here with me," Sally countermanded, not about to let her sister suffer the role of whipping boy.

"What? Even the worm turns," was jeered at

Jane who shrank behind Graham as Lady Ellen passed by.

Then she was gone, leaving behind a bleak emptiness that drained away the strength Sally had somehow managed to hang on to during the horrible confrontation. She started to shake.

"Anything I can do for you, Sally?" Graham asked caringly.

Her mind felt too scattered to think straight anymore. She needed comfort. "Would you ask Jeanette to bring us a pot of tea, please, Graham?"

"Sure."

He left the two sisters together. Sally held out her arms to Jane, who flew into the offered embrace, hugging her tight and bursting into tears. "It's okay," she automatically soothed. "We have each other. Whatever the future holds, we'll always have each other."

Right now the future felt like a blank slate.

But it wasn't really.

Jack Maguire was written on it.

This had been his day of reckoning.

Hers and Jane's, too.

She wondered how the slate would read in a year's time, but was too worn-out to think about it. Just take one day at a time, she told herself, do what feels right. Even when Jack Maguire comes to visit, I won't do anything that doesn't feel right.

CHAPTER SIX

JACK Maguire stood at the lounge room window of his Woolloomooloo apartment, watching the Queen Mary 2 make its majestic way down Sydney Harbour. It was accompanied by a flotilla of small craft which were made to look absolutely tiny by the massive cruise ship. Quite an incredible spectacle, Jack thought, and bound to bring out crowds of spectators on this, the new Queen Mary's first visit to Sydney.

His mind drifted to another first visit—one which he expected to be more personally satisfying. It had been two weeks since the contract with Sally Maguire had been signed, and she hadn't called him for help on any problem. He'd given her his cell-phone number but not once had she used it. Was she intent on proving herself capable of any task or was she shying clear of him?

Lady Ellen would have tried her best to poison her mind against him, but Lady Ellen had left the Yarramalong property the morning after the reading of the will. Couldn't bear to stay there with Sir Leonard gone, he'd heard on the social grapevine. Not a word about eviction. She was currently being cosseted as a house-guest of a high-society friend, playing the grieving widow and saving pride by pretending she'd left Sally to manage the property with her horses.

The silence from Yarramalong niggled him. Had Sally agreed to her mother's pretence, intent on keeping him out of their lives as long as she could? He didn't care what Lady Ellen said or did, provided *she* was out of the picture he'd set up for himself. However he did want to know if Sally had actually thrown her lot in with him or was playing along with her mother's game of deceit.

Time to make contact with her, he decided, and smiled cynically over the rush of eagerness that charged through him. Lust could make a fool of a man, and Jack was determined on never becoming any woman's fool. The trick was to control his desire for Sally Maguire, not ever allow it to gain too much power over his thoughts or actions. Being master of his own fate was the prime directive of his life and he was not about to change it.

He forced himself to wait until after the dinner hour before he called her, anticipating she would definitely be in the house at that time—not out with her horses—and readily available to chat with him. Having armed himself with a relaxing glass of cognac, he settled into his favourite chair, made the connection to the Yarramalong property, and listened to the buzzing summons of the telephone, conscious of a buzz of excitement in his blood as he wondered how much she'd thought about him this past fortnight.

"Sally Maguire."

The blunt announcement gave nothing away except her name.

"Hello, Sally," he drawled, rolling that same name off his tongue with considerable relish. "It's Jack Maguire, calling to catch up with what's happening at your end."

"Oh!" A breathy gush of surprise, then a burst of anxious concern. "Was I supposed to give you weekly reports or something? I don't remember you saying so."

"I didn't. I hear Lady Ellen is in town. I take it she won't be coming back to the property?"

A pause, then still with a note of anxiety, "I'm not expecting her to. She took all her personal things. I don't think it would suit her to…to make trouble over the situation."

It was an astute point. Wrong image if the widow wanted to make golden hay with a second husband. "How much trouble did she make for you, Sally?" he asked, still wondering if she had agreed to some deceptive scenario with her mother behind his back.

He heard the slight huff of a deep breath being scooped in. "I don't want to talk about it," she said very firmly. "I stood my ground. Okay? Everyone who works here has chosen to stay on. We're doing fine. No problems."

I stood my ground.

Jack smiled over those fighting words.

There'd been trouble, all right, but Sally had not given in to her mother on anything. Definitely a strong backbone there. He liked that in her. It could very well add a lot of spice to getting her into bed with him. He didn't believe she would come easily. Which made the prospect of winning the pillow fight all the more exciting.

"Are you…are you planning to visit soon?"

Her hesitant question revealed a nervous apprehension about his presence on the property. He didn't want her afraid of him. That wasn't part of his plan at all. Better to settle any fears she had—possibly implanted by the venomous Lady Ellen—before they grew into an insurmountable block.

"Tomorrow," he decided. "It's Friday. I'll fly in about six-thirty tomorrow evening and spend the weekend evaluating the whole place."

"Tomorrow," she said weakly, as though in shock at how quickly he would be arriving on the scene.

"Okay with you?" he pushed.

"Yes. Yes, of course," she said in a rush, obviously determined not to be found at fault. "Six-thirty. I'll have the welcome mat ready."

"Thank you, Sally." He poured warmth into his voice. "I'll look forward to it."

Sally fiercely told herself she had no reason to feel any sense of panic. Everyone had worked hard all day to ensure everything was picture perfect for Jack Maguire's personal evaluation of his property. The cleaning ladies had the house spick and span. The gardener had trimmed the lawn. Jeanette, after a frenzy of food shopping, was cooking a special welcome-home dinner. It was almost six o'clock and the only problem she had was deciding what to wear.

Should she dress up as her mother had always insisted they do for her father? She wasn't a wife or a daughter to Jack Maguire, only an employee, and although he had expressed a wish to be welcomed as his father had, Sally couldn't help worrying if dressing up might encourage him to think she was his for the taking—*his grateful little mistress!*

She hated her mother's spin on the situation, didn't want to give it any credence, yet she couldn't quite banish it from her mind, having thought the same thing before she'd persuaded herself otherwise.

She should trust her own judgement. Her mother hadn't talked with Jack, as she had. He wanted the welcome mat out. Part of that was dressing up, as anyone would for an important visitor. Who more important than Jack in these circumstances? Besides, in her heart of hearts, she wanted to look attractive, which was why she'd already spent so long washing and drying her hair into a gleaming mass of partially tamed curls.

Smart-casual, she finally decided, pulling on white slacks and a wraparound top in green and black and white. The top had cap sleeves and the V-neckline wasn't low enough to show any cleavage, yet as she did up the ties at the side of her waist, she started worrying that he might see it as *invitational.* But if he had sex on his mind, it didn't really matter what she wore, did it? And time was running out. Stupid to keep dithering.

She slapped some make-up on to give her face some colour. No perfume. Definitely not perfume, which might be interpreted as enticing. Satisfied with looking fresh and re-spectable, and doing her best to ignore the nervous thumping of her heart, she headed for the lounge room where the ingredients for a martini were lined up on her father's bar, ready to be mixed. She would present him with one when he emerged from the helicopter. That part of the arrival ceremony was surely harmless.

Besides, a greeting drink was appropriate in the circumstances.

Jeanette came in with a carefully arranged plate of antipasta and laid it on the bar counter. "In case he's peckish before dinner," she said, anxious to please. "Graham's waiting in the kitchen. He'll come out and carry Mr. Maguire's bag to the guest room when the helicopter lands." She gave Sally a worried look. "Are you sure he won't want the master bedroom? We don't want to offend."

"I'll ask him when he gets here. It's easy enough to change, Jeannette," she said soothingly.

The housekeeper patted down her apron and primped her permed grey hair. She was in her fifties and on the plump side, being fond of her own baking, but she prided herself on always looking neat and tidy and Sally knew these actions were symptoms of an attack of nerves. Change was difficult for everyone, she thought, probably more so for older people.

"The antipasta looks delicious and Jack

Maguire will certainly appreciate the care you've put into dinner," Sally assured her. "Stop worrying, Jeanette."

She heaved a sigh then cocked her head in listening mode. "That's the helicopter coming. Good luck, Sally." Her kind brown eyes flashed approval. "You look very nice."

"Thanks. And thanks for all you've done to make Jack feel welcomed here."

"Got to make him happy to have this place to come to. I don't mind telling you I'd hate to leave. That cottage has been our home for so long…" Another big sigh before she bustled out, leaving Sally to put the last finishing touch—a spiked olive—to the martini.

The helicopter noise was louder now. It seemed to vibrate right through Sally, making her body feel quivery. She gripped the martini glass very firmly and concentrated on not spilling a drop as she forced her shaky legs to walk out to the patio overlooking the helipad. It was important for Jack to see her there, waiting to welcome him. She had to get this right. Other people depended on her making him feel good about holding on to this property. A year would not be enough for Jeanette. The housekeeper wanted to keep her home.

The moment she stepped outside, the whirling wind from the helicopter blades blew her hair into wild disarray. She should have tied it back instead of leaving it loose—not thinking ahead, but nothing she could do about it now. She held grimly on to the glass, waiting for the craft to settle before heading down the steps to meet Jack.

The engine was switched off. The blades slowed. The doors opened for both Jack and the pilot to emerge. Sally plastered a smile on her face and, moving with what she hoped looked like casual grace, descended to the helipad to greet the man who had so suddenly become a driving force in her life.

Jack alighted from the passenger seat with a broad smile on his face and an eager bounce in his step. Amazing what a lift it had been to see Sally waiting for him on the patio, the fiery halo of her hair blown into a wild sunburst by the incoming helicopter. His mind did take note that she was only doing what he'd asked of her, but the cynical aside in no way reduced his pleasure in seeing her.

"Welcome home, Jack," she called to him, pausing her approach as he strode towards her, holding out the martini she'd brought to give him.

He laughed, enjoying the black humour of the situation. This *home* had been bought, as Sally well knew. He had no emotional connection to it. The connection was to her, and she was simply fulfilling the role he had wickedly suggested. Doing it with class, too, looking country-fresh and beautiful in white and green. *She* belonged here. *He* had no sense of belonging to anywhere.

Yet as he took the offered drink, and felt desire for her firing through his blood, he was glad he'd come, even though the welcome had been paid for.

"Thank you, Sally," he said, his eyes keenly

sweeping hers for some sign of what she was feeling.

"How was your day?" she asked brightly, as though he'd only left her this morning.

"Busy," he drawled, amused by the fiction she was keeping up. "Yours?"

"Very busy." Her own lips twitched in amusement over the trite conversation. She gestured to the grey suit he wore. "You look as though you've come straight from a boardroom."

"I have." He waved to the helicopter pilot who was already on his way up to the house with Jack's bag. "Bill has to fly back to Sydney while there's still daylight, so time was tight. I thought I'd change into more relaxing clothes when I got here."

"Of course." Her gaze flickered with some anxious uncertainty. "I've had the guest quarters prepared for you, Jack. My...your... father's personal things are still in the master bedroom suite. I wasn't sure if you'd want some...some keepsake..."

"No." He felt himself bristling with rejection of all that had *not* been freely given him by his father. Nothing had been offered. He would take nothing.

"I'm sorry." Her hands flew out in apologetic appeal. "I should have asked when you called last night but I didn't think of it until today, and then I didn't want to bother you at work."

"Fair enough," he clipped out, annoyed that he'd made his anger obvious to her, determined to clamp down on it. "Let's go inside," he suggested, adopting a more pleasant tone. "You can show me the master suite on the way to the guest quarters and I'll decide what's to be done."

One thing was certain. He didn't want anything left in it to remind him of his father or the woman who had supplanted his mother and ensured that her husband's son was persona non grata in this house. *His* house now, and he would not be shut out of any room in it. He was not a guest. He was the owner, and own it he would.

These thoughts were marching through his mind as Sally led him inside, her back very stiff and straight, probably thinking she had upset him with her lack of foresight—bad management. He would reassure her later when this issue had been dealt with. He was not about to lay fault on her. It had only been two weeks since the funeral and no doubt she'd had a lot to contend with, handling other changes.

The front door opened to a spacious foyer. Cream tiles on the floor were bordered by a terracotta and dark brown pattern in a distinctly Roman style. Caesar entering his palace, Jack thought sardonically. On one side, opened double cedar doors revealed a rather masculine lounge room—dark brown leather chesterfield sofas, a sandstone fireplace big enough to accommodate burning logs. His father had clearly been lord and master here.

But not in the bedroom.

Having been led down a wide corridor, Jack was ushered into a room that Lady Ellen had obviously decorated to please herself. Everything was sensuously feminine: elegant rosewood furniture, a silk brocade bedspread printed with lush red and deep pink roses, bundles of rich cushions, thick dark red carpet, matching red silk curtains. A room for a bordello queen, he thought cynically. He couldn't imagine Sally on that bed. The colours were wrong for her. So was the whole style of the room.

She opened another door, waving him on to look at the rest of the suite. A glance to the left revealed a dressing room lined with two long rows of closed cupboards, their panelled doors painted in varying shades of jade green. A ceiling-to-floor mirror was at the end, reflecting his and Sally's presence. Her back was turned to it, her attention focussed in the opposite direction.

On the right was a bathroom which instantly met his approval—a very spacious shower, easily large enough for two, and an equally luxurious spa bath, encased in marble tiles with a vein of jade green running through them. This part of the suite was fine, once he got rid of the red carpet in the dressing room. And whatever possessions were still housed behind the cupboard doors.

"I *will* occupy this suite when it's refurbished," he said casually. "In the meantime, the guest quarters will be fine, Sally. You made the right decision for me. I'll have an interior decorator call you next week to make arrangements for seeing what the job will entail. Okay?"

"Yes." Her inner tension visibly eased into a smile of relief. "What do you want done with Dad's things?"

"Keep anything you'd like and give the rest to a charity. The Smith Family does good work. Try them."

She nodded.

"And you can tell Lady Ellen she can have her bedroom furniture and furnishings free of charge," he added mockingly. "I can see they belong to her."

A flush of embarrassment blazed across her cheeks. "I'll let her know."

"I hear she's taken up residence with Marion

Harley," he prodded, wanting to know how much contact Sally was having with her mother.

"She left instructions for her mail to be redirected there," came the flat reply, carefully strained of any emotion. "I don't know for how long. I guess the furniture could be put in storage…if she wants to keep it."

Jack gleaned a strong impression of distance. No sense of any closeness. A ruction had definitely taken place. How much that pained Sally he didn't know but it was abundantly clear she was getting on with her own life without her mother in her ear on any regular basis, and the prospect of calling her about the furniture was causing stress, not pleasure.

"On the other hand, you could just give it away to The Smith Family," he said carelessly. "It's irrelevant to me."

"I'll call her first," she said with a flash of determination. "I'd feel wrong about giving it away without…without any consultation."

Doing the right thing…

Yes, she had a strong sense of rightness, Sally Maguire. Which was undoubtedly at the core of why she had felt sympathetic towards his position in regard to the Maguire family. It also meant he was going to have to make her feel *right* about going to bed with him.

This realisation made her even more desirable. It would certainly be a novelty, having sex with a woman where the attraction was not bolstered by his wealth. Just an honest mating…because they wanted to. He simply had to bring out the wanting in Sally, overcome whatever reservations she had about giving in to it. Her guard was up at the moment, feeling her way with him.

"Okay. We've got that settled," he said, smiling to put her more at ease. "Let's move on to the guest quarters."

She nodded and quickly led him back to the corridor which bisected this wing of the house. "My room," she said, indicating a door on the left hand side. No offer to show it to him and he didn't push for it, respecting her privacy though he was curious about how personal it was—how much it would tell him about her. She passed swiftly by but paused at the next door, turning anxiously appealing eyes to his.

"This is Jane's room. Most of the time she's in Sydney, sharing an apartment with other students while she attends the University of Technology. She's in her last year of studying to be a nurse and wants to be a midwife eventually. Is it okay if she comes home…I mean visits me…" she hastily corrected, "…when she can?"

Jack seized the chance to confirm that the victimised sister had been rescued from her monster mother. "If Lady Ellen is supporting Jane, wouldn't she expect a grateful daughter to give all free time to her?"

Colour whooshed into Sally's cheeks. "I'm supporting Jane. You're paying me enough. I can do it."

They were fighting words. Jack got the impression she would defend that action to the death. The break from Lady Ellen was definitely complete. The adopted daughters would never kowtow to her again. He smiled, reaching up to gently stroke her hot cheek in a salute of approval.

"What you choose to do with your salary is your business, Sally. I'm glad to hear you're looking after your sister."

"Then you don't mind if she comes here?"

Her eyes were huge pools of green. For a moment Jack almost lost himself in their brimming emotion—the kind of caring he'd only ever known from his mother. Jane wasn't even Sally's birth sister, yet…an odd spurt of jealousy formed his reply.

"I have no objection to her coming here to be with you, but I'd prefer not to have her visits clash with mine." *Taking your attention away from me.*

He dropped his hand, separating himself from the bond shared by the two sisters. No way was he going to allow it to interfere with what he wanted from Sally. Compassion for a victim he barely knew went only so far.

"Thank you. I'll see that they don't," she said,

her gaze skidding away from his, which suggested a very acute consciousness of what was sizzling through his intentions where she was concerned.

Jack was sure she was every bit as sexually aware of him as he was of her. It all came down to timing, he thought, telling himself that patience would serve him well. This weekend was groundwork, learning the lay of the land so he made no mistakes when he played his hand. It was like a poker game, knowing when to check and when to raise the stakes. Winning was often a delicate balancing act. And having the right cards was going to be essential with Sally Maguire.

She showed him into the guest quarters: a comfortable sitting room equipped with a plasma television and a kitchenette, serving two bedrooms with ensuite bathrooms. His bag had been brought in and placed on a stool in one of the bedrooms. All the décor was inoffensively beige, brown and white. The only splashes of colour came from the fresh flowers in vases and a bowl of fruit on the coffee table—welcoming touches. The one thing missing from the sense of being in a classy hotel was a bottle of champagne in an ice bucket. But he had been presented with a martini.

Sally made a quick departure, saying, "I'll leave you to get settled. Join me in the lounge room when you're ready."

No friendly lingering.

No availability signals.

"Thank you," he said to her fast retreating back, silently vowing this was the last time she would treat him as a guest.

He intended to be much more than that in Sally Maguire's life. Before this weekend was over, the distance she was trying to keep between them was going to be considerably lessened and the connection he felt with her re-asserted.

CHAPTER SEVEN

HE MADE no move on her.

All weekend…not the slightest suggestion of a move.

For much of it Sally had been racked with tension, expecting him to act on the pull of attraction she was unable to hide. When he had made her laugh over dinner on Friday night, his vivid blue eyes twinkling an appreciative tease as he remarked on Jeannette's delicious veal dish being the perfect offering of the fatted calf for the prodigal son; in the stables on Saturday morning after an exhilarating ride; relaxing on sunlounges after a swim in the pool when she couldn't help admiring his athletic physique, sleek-wet masculinity glistening, urging a desire to touch.

So many moments of acute vulnerability on her part—a dangerous electricity racing through her veins—and she knew he was aware of her reaction to him. His eyes simmered with his knowledge of it, a silent satisfaction that seemed to hum around her, yet not once did he take advantage of it, nor even speak of it.

If he wanted her as his "grateful little mistress," his lack of action on that front made no sense. Unless he was content to wait, get to know her better, enjoy building up her anticipation of what it might be like with him. Or maybe he didn't want *that* with her at all, just a place to come home to now and then without any sexual complications.

He'd given her a fleeting thank-you kiss on the cheek before leaving in the helicopter, certainly nothing to get fussed about. Yet after he'd gone, she couldn't settle to doing anything, wandering around the house, thinking about him until Jeanette called her for dinner, a light informal meal of quiche and salad in the kitchen, more than enough after the long, sumptuous lunch she'd shared with Jack.

"He's charming," Jeanette declared. "Lovely manners. A real gentleman. I don't know why Lady Ellen took against him." Then with an arch look at Sally, "And very handsome, too, I must say."

"Sensible chap," Graham chimed in approvingly. "Took an interest in everything. Got himself a thorough understanding of what's involved in running this place."

They liked him. There'd been nothing not to like. He'd taken the time to have long chats with both Graham and Tim Fogarty who'd been the groom for Sally's horses for years and lived in a self-contained apartment attached to the stables. Any worries the staff had about Jack's takeover had been completely allayed this weekend. He'd assured himself of a ready welcome by all of them any time he chose to visit in the future, though that wouldn't be for a while.

"I won't come back until the redecorating is done," he'd told her.

Sally didn't know how quickly his interior decorator would accomplish the changes in the master bedroom, but she figured it would probably take a few weeks. It was stupid to feel so…so let down by the fact that Jack was not hot to trot with her. He had a busy life in the city, maybe a woman who meant more to him there, a beautiful woman who was sharing a bed with him on a regular basis. No need for a *country* mistress.

She should be feeling relieved by the lack of sexual pressure from him, glad that her mother had been wrong. At least, when Jane telephoned her somewhat anxiously at eight o'clock, Sally had nothing bad to report.

"Has he gone?" came the first whispered question, as though Jack might overhear.

"Yes. He flew out at five-thirty."

"Are you all right, Sally? He didn't…"

"No. Nothing like that," she assured her sister. "As Jeannette remarked, Jack Maguire was a real gentleman. And Graham and Tim were very impressed with the interest he took in everything to do with the property."

A huge sigh of relief. "I've been so worried all weekend. After what Mum said about his intentions…"

"I told you there was no need to worry. I can handle myself, Jane. The showjumping scene is loaded with womanisers and I'm well practised at fending them off." Easy when you don't find *them* attractive. "Anyway, Jack didn't give me a problem. On the contrary, he even took a copy of the upcoming showjumping events I want to enter and said he would time his visits not to interfere with my schedule. And it's okay with him for you to visit me here."

She didn't add the rider—not when he was in residence—because it was easy enough to make arrangements which didn't clash with his time at the property, and Jane would only start worrying about his intentions again.

"He sounds…nice."

Nice was not a word Sally could apply to Jack Maguire. Her instincts were sensing a dark power in him which he kept leashed until the opportune moment came to unleash it. Just being with him filled her with a nervous excitement which was impossible to ignore or control.

"I wish Mum had let him into our lives," Jane went on ruefully. "It's not knowing him that's been the worry."

"Well, at least he doesn't feel vengeful towards us, Jane."

"No. Obviously not. He's being very generous. I just don't understand why, when we've done nothing for him."

"Maybe I'm doing it for him now, making him feel welcome here."

Jane heaved a sigh. "I hope that's all it is, Sally."

"Stop worrying. How's everything at your end? Has Mum been in touch?"

"No. You?"

"No. But I'll have to call her."

She explained about Jack wanting the master

bedroom redecorated to his taste and they chatted on, trying to fill the void of having lost the family situation they had been accustomed to all their lives, holding tightly to their sister-hood. Their parents were no longer there to influence or support them. They had to hang on to each other, though Sally couldn't confide her feelings about Jack Maguire to Jane, which made her feel very alone. Nevertheless, she'd chosen this route into her future—the *best* route since she could help her sister—so she had to stick with it. Besides, they were probably foolish feelings, anyway.

She did her best to forget them in the weeks leading up to the Maitland Show where she'd be competing in two showjumping events, the main one giving points towards securing a place in the World Cup team. Training her horses up to peak performance level kept her busy and focused on what was important to her.

On the home front she organised a removalist to take the bedroom furniture her mother wanted stored for future use. Jack's interior decorator came in, took a lot of measurements, had the red carpet taken up and carted away, brought in a tradesman to repaint the walls and promised to notify Sally when the new carpet, curtains and furniture would be installed.

Jack did not contact her personally, nor did she contact him. He knew about the Maitland Show and she had no qualms about loading up the horse truck and heading off for the weekend with Tim Fogarty, who always helped her with the horses on these excursions, feeding them, grooming them, setting up the exercise pen and generally seeing they were ready for her to ride. Tim was in his fifties, an experienced stable hand who'd once worked for a racehorse trainer. There was nothing he didn't know about horses, and Sally had a comfortable relationship with him, always respecting whatever advice he gave her.

There was accommodation for him at one end of the horse truck and she stayed at a local motel, usually booked out by other riders wanting a bit of social life in between training and competing. This time she planned to keep to herself, avoiding the gossipy crowd and their inevitable curiosity about the outcome from her father's death. Most of them would imagine she was an heiress, and they'd be all agog if she had to explain her real situation. It was none of their business and she didn't need that kind of distraction when she was competing.

As it was she had to deal with expressions of sympathy, but the aloof air she maintained protected her from more personal approaches. Until after she won a third place with her second-string horse and George Ponsonby decided she'd be in a more accessible mood with this success under her belt.

She'd no sooner dismounted and handed the horse over to Tim than George pounced, giving her a playful smack on the backside and flashing his whiter than white smile, designed to curl the toes of any female fool enough to fall for his boyish good looks and Casanova charm. Having competed in two Olympic Games, he was a fixture on the showjumping scene, and at thirty, had already been married and divorced twice to heiresses who'd found him cheating on them. Apparently she was his next target, no longer having a protective father in the picture.

"Great seat, Sally! How about plonking it on me tonight? I'm available. Good time guaranteed. Though since you must now be rolling in scads of money, you can shout for the drinks."

Before she could draw breath enough to pour scorn on his arrogant confidence, another voice cut in, a hard challenging voice that brooked no opposition.

"Miss Maguire is not available tonight. She will be dining with me."

Jack!

The shock of seeing him kicked her heart and left her mouth agape. George was stunned, too, not expecting to be challenged on what he considered his stamping ground. They both stared at Jack as he strolled forward to claim her company, taller than George and strongly emitting the dark power Sally associated with him—not a man to be thwarted on anything he aimed for.

Did George feel it, too?

He backed off fast. "Sorry. Didn't know Sal was spoken for," he gabbled and shot off to find easier game for a roll in the hay.

Jack paused to watch him flee the scene, surrendering the contest without so much as a backward glance, then cocked a sardonic eyebrow at Sally. "Just trying it on, was he?"

She scooped in a quick breath to relieve the tightness of her chest, which was being pummelled by a wild heartbeat. "George tries it on with every woman he fancies," she answered dryly. "He's incapable of keeping his trousers zipped."

"No serious attachment," Jack concluded.

"Never has been. Never will be with him," Sally said, shrugging to show the situation with George was totally unimportant and not worth discussing. "What are you doing here, Jack?"

"Came to watch you compete." His eyes drilled hers. "Am I in the way of some other attachment you have?"

"No. The riders are a fairly incestuous group. They tend to use sex as a bit of relaxation after the heat of competition. I don't like that kind of meaningless intimacy so I steer clear of it."

Why she was pouring out this intimate information she didn't know. Somehow it seemed important for him to understand she was very discriminating about whom she shared a bed with.

"So you don't sleep around on the showjumping circuit."

Sexy satisfaction in his voice.

A wave of heat ran through her. "I'm not an easy lay anywhere, Jack," she flashed at him, suddenly feeling he might be measuring her for his bed and not wanting him to think she would just fall into it with him at his bidding.

He smiled, not the least bit put out by her aggressive statement, amused by her need to make it. "I can get an easy lay any time I want one,

Sally. That's not what brought me to this show today. I simply wanted to see you doing your thing, and I was about to congratulate you on your third place when George's familiarity with you distracted my intention."

Confusion swirled over the sexual tension he raised in her. Most probably his interest was simply…interest. Something new. Something different from the life he usually led. She took a deep breath to feed some clearing oxygen into her muddled mind and managed a smile back at him.

"Well you certainly dealt with that effectively. I've never seen George so completely intimidated."

He laughed. "I was offended on your behalf. Not only was the guy a groper but a freeloader, as well."

Offended…

She looked at him consideringly. "So that was your protective big-brother act?"

"No." His grin set her hormones buzzing again. "That was me wanting you to myself." He waved towards the refreshment van. "I thought we could have a coffee together before your next event."

"I'd rather have a long cold drink." She was hot, and not just from competing in the show ring.

"Whatever you like," he said equably.

She took off her riding helmet and ran her fingers through her hair as they moved towards the van. He watched her fluff out the rioting curls with a sensual little smile on his lips.

"Can't blame George for finding you sexy," he remarked admiringly. "Your hair is like a beacon on top of that figure-hugging navy jacket, not to mention the fawn pants fitting the bottom half of you like a second skin."

Which made her acutely aware of her body and its quivery response to his highly male sex appeal, heightened by the black jeans and black T-shirt he wore, the force of his personality making every other man totally insignificant.

"It's the official outfit," she answered defensively. "And let me tell you George's interest is more in my inheritance than me. Except I haven't got one. And you butted in before I could correct his assumption."

"Ah! Tricky business having bags of wealth behind you." His eyes twinkled with wicked teasing. "At least you'll know from now on you're wanted for yourself."

Was there desire for her simmering behind that twinkle? Her mind whirled with the frustration of not knowing, then seized on the chance to find out more about him. "What about you, Jack? Are there lots of women panting for what you've got? How do you sort them out?"

He shrugged. "Sooner or later that issue sorts itself out."

The cynicism in his voice prompted her to ask, "You've never wanted to marry?"

He slid her a look that cut straight to her heart. "Are you angling to marry me, Sally?"

It shocked her into stopping dead. Agitated by his thinking it was possible, even probable, she swung to confront him with a rush of anguished protest. "No! Don't ever think that! I'm not like my mother! I wouldn't ever try to trap you or…or…"

His mouth curled sardonically. "So Lady Ellen suggested it."

The certainty in his eyes made it impossible to deny. She had the sickening sense that he'd known it, anyway, known before she'd blurted out the too-revealing words about her mother. Her cheeks burned with the humiliating truth.

"What was the plan?" he bored in. "Lure me to your bed and get yourself pregnant?"

She grimaced at the accuracy of his deduction. "She said you had to want me or you wouldn't have set up the situation with me at the property, and I could secure my future by…by giving you whatever you wanted and…and trapping you into fatherhood." Her eyes begged his belief. "But I'd never have a baby for that reason, Jack. Please…don't think I would."

Had he been thinking it? Was that why he'd kept his distance from her?

"And I wouldn't marry anyone for money," she added vehemently. "I want…"

"What do you want, Sally?" he pushed.

She heaved a huge sigh and gave up her heart-felt truth. "I want there to be love between me and the man I marry. A deep and abiding love."

"And while you're waiting for this love—" he lifted a hand and gently stroked her burning cheek, an ironic little smile playing on his lips "—will you fill in the time with me?"

What did he mean?

Love and marriage had nothing to do with any relationship they might have.

He was being very clear on that.

But how did he envisage filling the present gap in her life?

"Did you set all this up just to have sex with me, Jack?" she blurted out, driven by the need to get the situation absolutely straight in her mind.

He mused over the question for several moments before answering, "No. I wanted to know you, Sally Maguire," he said on a wryly whimsical note. "Know all about you…the way you live your life. Which is why I'm here, watching you compete."

The way she lived her life…as the adopted daughter of his father…the life he might have had if he hadn't been taken away from it. Kept away.

The injustice to him tugged at her emotions again. She wanted to give him what he hadn't had, wanted to give him the sense of belonging. He stirred so many desires in her, and the bottom-line truth was she didn't want to shut him out on any level. *Open the door, Sally,* she fiercely told herself, *and let him in.*

"Do you mind?" he asked quietly. "I really enjoyed seeing you ride. It even made me groan in sympathy when your horse knocked the top rail on the triple jump. You were right on the time clock to win if he'd sailed clear. But if you find my interest disturbing…"

"No," she answered quickly.

"Then will you share the excitement of your day over dinner with me tonight?"

"Yes. I'd like that," she said decisively. "Thank you."

It was an opportunity to learn more about him, too. Knowing this man—all that he was, how he lived *his* life—seemed more important than anything else.

He nodded. "A pleasure I'll look forward to."

Then he smiled.

It was a smile that swept the dark churning clouds right out of her mind, replacing them with a tingling anticipation for the time they would spend together.

CHAPTER EIGHT

"SALLY MAGUIRE riding Midnight Magic…"

It WAS the last event of the day, the most important event for those competing. Not only did it carry the largest prize money, but points would be awarded in the scoring system used to select the team for the World Cup.

From his seat in the grandstand, Jack leaned forward to watch Sally ride the big black gelding into the show ring. Midnight Magic was her top-level horse, the one she'd been training up to this standard for the past five years. It was a magnificent animal, its mane and tail plaited, its gleaming coat brushed into a checkerboard pattern. Tim Fogarty had groomed it beautifully—an absolute stand-out horse—but it was performance not looks that won this event.

Jack couldn't remember the last time he'd felt nervous about an outcome. Probably back in his poker days when it was impossible to control what cards would turn up on the table and he needed to win, needed big money fast so he could play in his father's arena. Right now he wanted Sally to win but he couldn't make it happen. It was up to her and the horse. Nevertheless, he found himself willing her to ride faultlessly, willing it so fiercely it surprised him that he cared so much.

And it wasn't because it would put her in a good mood afterwards, easier for him to move closer to her. The desire that had spurred him along this road had been somewhat derailed by other factors; the sheer entertainment of her company—such a fresh outlook on life and so straight-line it commanded his respect. She made the sophisticates in his social set totally boring in comparison. He didn't want to spoil her world, yet the desire she stirred in him was so damned strong, playboy George had been in danger of being flattened if he'd kept his lecherous hands on her.

Mine...

He shook his head over the mad spurt of possessiveness that had seized him. Bad enough that the urge to be with her again had made waiting for the redecorating to be done intolerable. She was turning his world upside down. He'd actually spoken the truth when she'd asked him whether he'd bought her for sex. It *had* been his initial motivation, yet the more he was with her, the more he did want the whole experience of Sally Maguire, not just her body pleasuring his.

The starter gun went off. She set Midnight Magic into a controlled stride towards the first jump. Jack felt his stomach clenching as the horse lifted and cleared the hurdle. His breath whooshed out in relief. *Go, girl, go...*his mind chanted as she rode around the course, fault free. He kept an eye on the time clock. The seconds were ticking by. The horse rattled the rail on the water obstacle—was she taking him too fast? The big triple was coming up. If the pacing was wrong, the horse might baulk at the wall.

Jack was on his feet, unable to sit still as she moved into the approach to the triple, ahead of the previous rider on the clock. The lift and the landing for the first two jumps had to be right, the paces in between perfectly measured. His heart was pumping hard as he watched Midnight Magic soar over all three cleanly, then gallop to the finish line.

She'd done it!

Beaten every other rider so far.

He clapped so hard his hands hurt. She looked up at the grandstand, saw him. He gave her a high five and she returned it, her lovely face lighting up with a brilliant smile. She rode out of the ring and he sat down again, smiling himself over the shared moment of exhilaration. There were two more riders to go but she'd done well and he was happy for her.

* * *

The winner!

Joyful triumph was thumping through Sally's heart as the judge hung the blue ribbon around Midnight Magic's neck. She scanned the grand-stand for Jack but couldn't spot him. He'd moved from where he had been, probably coming to congratulate her. She'd achieved a couple of thirds at this level, but never a first, and it wouldn't have been possible without Jack's support. She wanted to thank him, wanted…oh, she was filled with so many wants, her body was buzzing with them.

He was waiting for her just beyond the gate, chatting with Tim Fogarty, both of them grinning their delight in her success. She virtu-ally leapt off her horse in her eagerness to join them. Tim came forward to take the reins and lead Midnight Magic away.

"Great riding, Sally. Mr. Maguire's just been telling me he's taking you off for a celebratory dinner and I got to say you deserve it. Leave the horses to me. I'll take care of them and get them home. You go and enjoy yourself."

"Thanks, Tim. I'll have to change my clothes in the truck first."

"I'll be here for a while. No hurry. Give me your helmet and I'll put it away."

She quickly unclipped it, handed it over, then, still brimming over with excitement, she turned to Jack. He spread his arms as though saying, "Look at you—a blue ribbon winner!" and she couldn't stop herself from hurtling into a hug. He lifted her up and swung her around, laughing at her happy exuberance, sharing it.

"That's the best I've ever done!" she cried as he set her on her feet again. "Thank you for making it possible, Jack."

"I'm glad I did," he said, his vivid blue eyes sparkling with warm pleasure.

"I felt you watching me. I had to do well, show you I was worth supporting," she babbled on.

"I was willing you over every jump."

"It was like I had wings."

He laughed, the sparkle in his eyes gathering

a wicked tease. "You had a dark angel riding on your shoulder."

She sighed, frowning at his description of himself. "I don't want you to be dark, Jack."

His mouth quirked into a musing little smile as he surveyed the earnestness on her face. "Maybe I need your sunshine in my life, Sally Maguire."

"Yes," she agreed, happy with the idea that she could answer a need in him that had nothing to do with sex. Somehow it helped to even out all he was giving her and made their connection more important. Though, having her breasts pressed to the hard wall of his chest and her thighs brushing up against the strong muscularity of his was making her very sexually aware of him. She slid her hands down from his shoulders, easing back from his embrace as she voiced her thought. "I'd like to think I could make a difference to all that's gone before. I'm sorry you were left so…so alone. It must have made you feel very dark."

"At times," he admitted. "But not right now. This is definitely a champagne moment." He dropped his embrace, took one of her arms and tucked it snugly around his. "Let's get on our way and have ourselves a fine dinner."

It was the best evening of Sally's life.

Jack had driven up to Maitland in his BMW convertible and he put the hood down before they took off for the Hunter Valley vineyards where there were dozens of fine restaurants. It felt great, zooming along the road in his beautiful car, her hair fluttering in the lovely cooling breeze, Jack tossing her amused smiles as she rattled off a whole lot of showjumping stories, continually prompting her to tell him more, enjoying her company, exciting her with the warm interest in his eyes.

He handled the powerful car with brilliant ease. She couldn't help watching his hands moving on the steering wheel, controlling the gearstick—so competent, confident—and wondered what it would feel like to have them touching her. Her gaze was drawn again and again to his powerful thighs flexing against the

stretch denim of his jeans as he braked or accelerated. He oozed a maleness that had her
stomach clenching over the thought of seeing
him naked, feeling him naked.

Wicked thoughts.

Dangerous thoughts.

Yet she couldn't stop them from sliding into
her mind, no matter how sternly she told herself
that love and marriage was not on his agenda
and it would be foolish to succumb to a physical
affair where she would most probably end up
craving more than he was prepared to give of
himself. Not only that, it would change their
current arrangement, maybe spoil it. On the
other hand, it was impossible to ignore what
she was feeling with him.

They stopped at Kirkton Park, a beautiful
holiday resort in the middle of vineyard country.
Having collected glasses of champagne from
the bar, they strolled out to the rose garden—all
red roses, scenting the air. They sat on one of the
garden benches, enjoying the delightful

ambience as they sipped the celebratory drink in the twilight of this wonderful day.

Sally queried Jack on the work that was occupying his business life and he talked openly of the problems he was sorting out in the transport industry, revising the truck drivers' schedules so that none of them had to take drugs to stay awake on unreasonably long hauls. "My father cut too many corners in his drive for maximum profits, always intent on expanding his empire. He didn't care about his people," he explained, and suddenly the darkness was back, brooding behind his eyes.

Impulsively Sally reached over and squeezed the hand resting on his thigh. "I'm glad you care, Jack."

He turned his hand to take hers, his strong fingers lacing through her fingers, gripping, transmitting a heat that ran up her arm and spread through her entire body. "It's easier not to," he said mockingly. "Caring eats into you."

Like the caring that had brought him back to Australia, the caring that had driven him to command his father's attention, the caring that had demanded retribution for how he had been treated. Sally understood exactly what he meant.

"It's in your nature to care," she said quietly, certain it was true. "You're not like your father. Nor my mother," she added ironically, lifting her gaze to show her empathy for all he had felt.

He shook his head, regarding her curiously. "How did the person you are survive in that household, Sally?"

She shrugged. "I learnt to play the role expected of me. Until you changed everything."

His grimace expressed a sudden burst of intense distaste. "When I fly in next time, you don't have to meet me with a martini," he said gruffly. "Just be yourself. Okay?"

"Okay."

She smiled.

Then abruptly he was on his feet, drawing her up from the garden bench, his voice a low burr, announcing, "I'm hungry. Let's go eat."

He held on to her hand. Sally's feet wanted to

dance all the way inside to the restaurant. She could barely keep a lid on the coiled springs in her legs. He liked the person she was. He wanted her in his life. Her mind bubbled with a wild happiness. She wanted him in her life, too. It felt right.

They ordered a meal and ate it, washing it down with a glass of fine chardonnay. Everything tasted delicious. Jack talked about life on his stepfather's ranch, competing in rodeos when he was a teenager. Sally hung on every word, fascinated that horses had played such a big part of his younger years, loving the fact that he'd been so attuned to her riding in the show ring today.

She should have been revelling in the pleasure of being with him on the drive home to Yarramalong, but somewhere along the way she drifted off to sleep, the huge energy drain of the day catching up with her. Consciousness returned with a jolt—an arm sliding under her knees, words murmured in her ear.

"Come on, Sleeping Beauty. Lift your arms

around my neck and I'll carry you in to your room."

"What…?"

"We're home."

While still befuddled, she was hoisted up out of the passenger seat of the car, her arms instinctively flinging themselves over his shoulders for extra support. "Jack…I can walk." It was a half-hearted, foggy protest. Her body didn't want to cooperate with it at all and did nothing to assert its independence, perfectly content to be cradled against his warm chest.

"Just relax, Sally," he instructed, and it was so nice simply to do as she was told, dropping her head onto his shoulder, her face pressing close to the strong column of his neck, breathing in the heady male scent of him—cologne, shampoo…she didn't know what but he smelled good.

Home, she thought dizzily, until a practicality struck her. "Door key."

"Got it in my hand," he assured her.

She sighed, happy that he'd thought of everything. The house was undoubtedly empty by now, but Jeanette would have left lights on in the foyer and hall before heading off to her cottage with Graham. No problem for Jack to negotiate his way inside. He wasn't even breathing heavily from carrying her. So strong…

She supposed Tim had passed on the news that she'd be coming home later with Jack. One of the guest suites would have been made ready for him. That was no problem, either. Except she wanted to keep holding on to him. Her nerves were humming with the pleasure of being this close.

The front door was opened and shut behind them.

Across the foyer.

Down the hall.

Sally's heart drummed harder with each step Jack took towards her bedroom. The drowsy languor was gone. She was wide-awake and acutely aware of fast approaching the moment of parting, wantonly wishing it didn't have to be so.

He opened her door.

Left it open.

She felt his muscles tense as he moved towards the bed, which was visible from the light in the hall. He was going to lay her down and leave. She knew it and inwardly screamed at his gentlemanly restraint.

Put her down and go, Jack savagely told himself. Sally was trusting him to do just that. He'd brought this raging desire upon himself, gratifying some caveman instinct by carrying her—*his woman.* It wasn't her fault that the softness of her breasts against his chest was making his heart pound harder, that her breath against his throat was an almost unbearable tease. He wanted the heat of her mouth pressed to his skin, but she hadn't done it. Any other woman he'd been with would have, showing her own desire for the sexual connection he craved. But Sally…

Just put her down and let her go to sleep on a happy day.

He forced himself to lean over and lay her gently on the bed. Her arms did not slide away. They remained locked around his neck. He looked down at her face, seductively framed by the spill of red-gold curls on the white pillow. Her eyes weren't closed. They were wide-open, mutely appealing, striking straight at the heart of the desire he'd been trying to contain, rendering it impossible to resist.

It wasn't a light kiss. It wasn't a "sweet-dreams, good-night" kiss. His mouth fell upon hers with ravaging passion, the pent-up urges of many weeks driving him to take all she was willing to give. And her response was equally wild and fierce, hands raking through his hair, holding his head to hers as her mouth accepted and returned his plunder, deeply intimate, intensely exciting.

He wasn't even conscious of moving onto the bed with her. He felt her body straining against his, the whole gorgeous length of her femininity seeking the feel of him. He wrapped his arms around her, hugging tightly. She hooked a leg over his. They kissed with a feverish madness that consumed any rational thought. There was only need answering need, revelling in the mutual hunger for each other.

"Clothes off," he rasped as he broke from her mouth to draw breath, his hand already under her T-shirt, unclipping her bra.

"You, too," she demanded, levering herself up, tearing at his shirt.

They dragged off everything, hurling each unwanted garment out of the way, the need to be free of any barriers between them driving a haste that allowed no sense of inhibitions. They came together again, skin against skin, soft flesh moulding itself to his hardness, generating more heat, more hunger.

His mind was awash in sensation. His body knew only intense urgency. She was ready for him, hot, moist, welcoming, and he plunged inside her, revelling in feeling her convulse around him. He kissed her again, his tongue driving deeply into her mouth. Hers pushed into his, passionately repeating his invasion. Her legs wrapped around his hips, her body lifting, arching, wanting him to pump himself into her.

He was completely out of control, his heart thundering with the rhythm of their bodies thrusting for the ultimate peak of pleasure, exulting in the excitement as they raced towards it. He felt her tension break into quivering, heard her cry out, and his own explosive release gushed from him in violent spasms, and a deep, guttural cry burst from his throat.

He held her to him with a fierce possessiveness, and they lay together, still intimately joined, their legs entwined, slowly getting their breath back, pulse rates calming down, luxuriating in the sense of intense togetherness. Her head was tucked under his chin. His fingers savoured the silk of her hair. He smelled it, kissed it, tasted it, loved it. Her skin was like

silk, too. He felt intoxicated by the glorious sen-
suality of her lovely curvy body. Another time
he would kiss her all over, but right now he just
wanted to hold her.

She fell asleep on him.

He didn't mind.

It showed she wasn't worried about what
they'd done.

Or was happy about the possibility of
getting pregnant.

A wave of cold sanity washed through him.

He'd lost his head in a blaze of lust.

He hadn't used protection.

CHAPTER NINE

SALLY awoke to the steadily insistent buzz of the telephone. The memory of last night with Jack crashed straight into her mind with the consciousness of being naked. Her head whipped around on the pillow to check if he was still with her. No. The telephone kept demanding her attention. She grabbed for the receiver on the bedside table and was shocked to see her alarm clock read 9:07. She'd slept almost ten hours!

"Sally Maguire," she said sharply, realizing that Jeanette would be in the kitchen by now and had put the call through to her room.

"It's Jack."

The sound of his voice sent a thrill through her. She smiled and lay back down, her free hand automatically stroking down her stomach, recalling the intense pleasure he'd given her, the incredible sensations. "I just woke up."

"So did I."

"Where are you?"

"In my Sydney apartment."

"Why didn't you stay?"

"I have an appointment for lunch today."

"Oh!" His life in the city…she tried to swallow her disappointment but it probably crept into her voice. "It was so wonderful…"

"I take it you're not sorry it happened."

"No." Impossible to be sorry. Hadn't she secretly wanted him all along?

"I didn't plan to finish off the night like that, Sally."

It was a statement of fact and she believed him, remembering how she had hung on to him, virtually inviting what had followed.

"And I forgot to use protection," he added pointedly.

It was like a knife to her heart. Was he thinking

she had lured him into her bed, pulling him into an intimacy with the intention of getting pregnant? Her whole body tensed with horror. Had he left when he'd realised what he'd done, repulsed by the idea he'd fallen into the trap her mother had laid out?

"Jack, it was safe! I swear to you it was!" she cried vehemently. "I'm on the pill!"

She hadn't planned last night, either, but the very day after her mother had left the property, she'd gone to her local doctor and got a prescription for the pill, determined not to be caught out if she did succumb to the strong attraction of Jack Maguire. She was *not* going to use a baby to tie him to her financially or any other way.

"Well, that should be safe enough." His voice had a sardonic ring to it as he added, "I'd hate you not to be fit for competing in the World Cup."

Relief poured through her. He didn't seem to be doubting her word. Nevertheless, the reference to her showjumping might mean he intended to distance himself from her, not risk getting trapped again. It took a huge effort to respond to him normally. "It's only the start of the season, Jack. I'll have to perform well at every event."

"Great start! I'm glad I was there to see it."

He did sound glad. Maybe she was over-reacting. Needing more assurance that all was well between them, she asked, "When will I see you again?"

"Probably next weekend. I'll let you know."

That sounded too casual, too vague. She'd be on tenterhooks until he did call her. She took a deep breath and tried to pour warmth into her voice. "I hope you have a good week, Jack, and thank you for making yesterday more special."

"You're a very special lady, Sally Maguire. 'Bye for now."

"'Bye," she echoed, then lay there in the bed he'd shared with her so intimately last night, holding the receiver to her thumping heart, hoping that being "a very special lady" did not set her apart in a bad way. She desperately wanted it to mean he believed her innocent of any rotten plotting and would make the effort to be with her again as soon as he could. A week was not very long, not when his business life was tied to the city.

She finally pushed herself to get up, shower, dress and present herself to the world Jack had allowed her to keep for a year because he wanted to experience her. Though whether he wanted to keep experiencing her was the burning question.

Jeanette was in the kitchen, as expected, drinking a cup of tea and reading a Sunday newspaper. She looked up as Sally entered. "Ah! Ready for breakfast?"

"Mmm. Big appetite, too." She felt terribly empty and very much in need of comfort food. "I'll have the lot this morning, bacon, eggs, fried tomato, mushrooms if we've got them."

"Coming up." Jeanette rose from her kitchen

stool to busy herself at the stove, throwing Sally a curious look. "Not like you to sleep in this long. I wouldn't have put that call through except it was Mr. Maguire."

Sally shrugged off the query, not wanting to explain too much. "Big day yesterday."

Jeanette smiled. "Tim told us you won the main event. Congratulations!"

"Thanks."

"And that Mr. Maguire was there to watch you, taking you out to dinner and bringing you home." This was delivered with an arch look.

"Yes. He did." Sally hitched herself onto the stool the housekeeper had vacated, trying to look casually relaxed.

"But he didn't stay," Jeanette pressed.

"No. He had to get back to Sydney. He was just calling to say he'll probably be here next weekend."

"I'll let everyone know." She fetched the breakfast items from the refrigerator while the frying pan was heating up and nodded to the coffee machine. "Pour yourself a cup. It's freshly made, ready for you."

"You spoil me, Jeannette." Sally tossed her a smile as she moved to help herself to coffee.

"You've always been a good girl," Jeannette said approvingly, then a pause before the probing comment, "Tim says Mr. Maguire is very taken with you."

Her heart lifted at hearing the observation, but if Jack believed he had been taken *by* her…she savagely wished this pregnancy issue had never come up.

"I like him, too. Very much," she answered.

It drew a look of anxious concern. "Do you think it will be all right, Sally? I mean…it's sort of complicated with the property and all."

It was a sobering point of view, and a valid one. What would happen if the relationship between her and Jack fell apart, if his interest in her was satisfied faster than Sally cared to think about? Like right now!

"I don't know, Jeanette," she answered, trying

to quell a sudden rush of panic at the thought of being abandoned because she'd wanted him to love her. "Whatever happens between us, I don't believe for a minute Jack would break the contract we've signed, so we can count on being here for the full year." With him, or without him.

"Yes. There's that. And who knows?" She threw Sally a hopeful smile. "Maybe it will work out very happily."

That was well and truly a pipedream at the moment, but Sally couldn't bring herself to throw a wet blanket over it. She was head-over-heels in love with the man. Even though he'd told her straight out that love and marriage was not on his agenda, people could and did change their minds. Last night, the deep connection she had felt with him had consumed any concern she might have had over doing something wrong. If he had felt it, too…

"Where did you have dinner?" Jeannette asked.

Relating that experience was easier than answering questions about Jack—questions she didn't know the answers for anyway. The dinner at Kirkton Park and the showjumping filled the rest of the conversation over breakfast.

Then Jane rang, wanting to know if she'd scored for the World Cup, and she relived the excitement of her success for her sister. It kept playing through her mind whether or not to tell Jane *everything* that was happening. They'd never kept secrets from each other. Yet she didn't want to hear a whole lot of worrywart stuff, which the confiding of her feelings for Jack Maguire would inevitably draw because of their mother's poisonous view of the situation.

It was Jane who finally brought him up. "Do you know when to expect another visit from Jack?"

"He called this morning to say he'd probably come next weekend," she answered, trying to sound matter-of-fact and feeling awkward about not sharing.

It was too new, she argued to herself. And it might have already ended for Jack. If he did come next weekend, and he left her still feeling like this about him, she would tell her sister then and deal with the gush of concern.

"Is it okay if I come to visit, too?" Jane asked. "I'd like to meet him on home ground."

Sally's chest instantly tightened. She didn't want Jane watching over her with Jack. It would be inhibiting. Besides, there was Jack's embargo on Jane's visits, as well.

"You can be with me as often as you like, but he doesn't want you here when he is, Jane," she stated flatly. "He said so from the start. Maybe he'll soften on that point as time goes on, but I think it's too soon to try changing the conditions he laid down."

A short, tense silence.

Sally felt miserably guilty for shutting Jane out, yet she didn't want family issues intruding on what was a very private and personal new experience for her.

"Does he think I sided with Mum at the solicitor's office?"

"I don't know," she answered quickly, too uncomfortable with the situation to discuss it. "I'll talk to him about it when the right opportunity arises. Okay?"

"I don't want to make trouble for you," came the typically anxious reply.

Sally sighed. "You won't, Jane. You never do. Just be happy doing your nursing course. I'll take care of everything at this end."

The assurance was enough to settle the problem. Temporarily. Sally knew she'd have to deal with it eventually, but having time alone with Jack was a far more pressing need.

The week passed in a flurry of activity, each day raising the hope that everything was still all right between them because there'd been no cancellation of the changes to the master suite.

On Monday the new carpet was laid. It was a deep jade green—deeper than the shades of green on the cupboard doors in the dressing-room—and so plush it felt like velvet underfoot.

The bedroom furniture arrived on Tuesday. The style was French Provincial, mostly ivory with decorative scrolls picked out in gold—a king-size bed, two bedside tables, a very elegant coffee table accompanied by two armchairs upholstered in a diamond pattern of dark jade, a much paler green and ivory in silk brocade with gold braiding around the edges.

Wednesday brought a plasma television, which was installed on the wall to the right of the door leading to the ensuite rooms, taking the place where her mother's dressing table had previously stood. Jack would have no use for a dressing-table, Sally thought, and the television suggested that he planned to visit frequently.

The rest of the furnishings came on Thursday: beautiful gold and ivory table lamps; bedlinen in dark-jade-green Egyptian cotton; a glorious bedspread in the same silk brocade used on the armchairs; a pile of rich cushions to decorate the bed. Dressing up the double glass doors that opened onto the pergola area outside were silk side curtains in the dark and light green, looped into a graceful drape with gold cord and tassles, an expanse of ivory organza in between, all hanging on a long gold rod with elaborate scrolls at both ends.

The whole effect was beautiful, but it was crowned by the magnificent painting that was carried in and positioned on the other side of the wall to the television set. Sally could hardly believe it was a real Monet—one of the great artist's paintings of waterlilies—but it was. It really was. Had to be worth millions of dollars, and Jack had chosen to have it hung here!

This couldn't be such a temporary thing for him. No-one would cart a Monet around frivolously. It complemented the furnishings perfectly, a wonderful highlight, but such a valuable painting had to mean he cared a great deal about wanting this to be a place that would give him a lot of pleasure, so surely he had to intend spending a lot of time at the property. With her.

He called that evening. "I'll be flying in at six o'clock tomorrow," he said without preamble.

"And I'll be waiting to greet you with a glass of

champagne," she trilled back at him, overflowing with a bubbling excitement she couldn't contain.

"Champagne?" he queried in an amused tone.

"Well, you don't want a martini, and I think the newly decorated master suite deserves to be christened with champagne."

"You like it?"

"I love it! They've done a wonderful job. And Jack…the Monet painting…it's so beautiful I have to keep going in to look at it."

He laughed. "One of my more extravagant investments. I'm glad you like it. I wanted you to enjoy it with me."

Sharing…caring…for a moment Sally was lost in those blissful thoughts. Then she realised Jack was probably thinking of enjoying the painting with her from the bed in the master suite. Was expecting to do so. Why not, after last Saturday night? It was a reasonable expectation.

Yet somehow—maybe it was the incredibly valuable Monet painting—the feeling of Jack having deliberately set out to make the master suite a temptingly seductive place to be, sent a chill through her mind. Was he using all he was capable of giving to ensure having what he wanted—keeping her captivated for as long as he was enjoying the experience of her? And having given so much, did that remove any guilt he might have about leaving her and moving on when he'd had enough?

She didn't really know how his mind worked. Except when he set a course of action, he followed it through with ruthless efficiency, doing whatever had to be done for the desired result. Easier not to care, he'd said, but there had to be caring behind the sheer drive of the man. Dark angel. Dark caring. Blackjack Maguire, taking over what his father had owned, what his father had put ahead of him…like her, the adopted daughter.

"Sally?"

"Yes?"

"What was that silence about?"

Boring straight in on her doubts, intent on stopping any retreat from him. It was too late to retreat anyway, Sally told herself, willing away the sense of being ruthlessly manipulated. "I was thinking…I've only been in your company for a few days."

"Time has nothing to do with the connection we have, Sally," he asserted confidently.

The connection…

He did feel it.

A dark burden lifted from her soul.

No matter what was hidden in the dark recesses of Jack's mind, the connection between them was real. And there could be no going back to maintaining a distance from him. Besides, she wanted to go forward, regardless of what happened further down the track.

"Six o'clock," she said, reminding him there was physical time involved.

He laughed as though that had no real relevance. "I'll bring a bottle of French champagne and we can toast the Monet together."

"I'll have the flute glasses ready. And an ice bucket."

On the coffee table in the master suite. Her heartbeat instantly accelerated at the thought. Was that too bold of her? No. What was the use of pretending she didn't want to spend every minute with him, anywhere, any time?

"I'll be living for the moment." His voice purred contentedly in her ear. "Good night, Sally."

"Good night to you, too," she answered, knowing she'd be living for the moment, as well.

Maybe this pleasure in each other wouldn't last, but as long as it did, she wasn't about to turn away from it.

CHAPTER TEN

IT WAS different, flying into the valley property this time. As the lush green pastures and the pristine white fences came into view, Jack felt a far more personal connection to the place. The sense of being an outsider, just coming in to take what he'd paid for, was no longer in play.

He didn't belong at this property but it belonged to him. He'd walked all over it, been accepted by the staff, and he was now well entrenched in the world that had once been his father's private domain. Mine now, he thought with satisfaction. And so was Sally—the daughter his father had prized far more than his son.

It had been a bad moment last week when he'd realised he'd forgotten to use a condom.

He'd had one in his wallet and it had been reck-lessly stupid of him not to keep control of what he was doing. Still, Sally was not a conniving bitch like her mother, and her being on the pill had saved him from a costly accident. Lady Ellen had been right about a pregnancy. He couldn't—wouldn't—walk away from his own child. Just as well Sally was as keen as he to avoid that consequence.

He smiled over her delight in the selections he'd made for the master bedroom suite. The re-styling had been for her—his vision of her oc-cupying it with him—but the Monet definitely made it his. Every time she looked at it, he would possess a piece of her mind.

His smile took on a twist of irony over the strong streak of possessiveness she had tapped in him. No other woman had got to him so deeply. Was it a psychological thing, rising out of the fact she'd had what he'd wanted all these years with his father, so having her balanced the ledger in some primal fashion?

Whatever…she certainly stirred something that was pushing him beyond the normal pattern of his experience with women. She wasn't simply a peripheral pleasure to be enjoyed when he had the time and inclination. It was difficult to banish her from his mind, even when he was doing business.

He hoped she was thinking of him just as much. The idea of her having a more powerful pull on him than he had on her was unacceptable. Holding the controlling hand and capitalising on it had made him the man he was, and he wasn't about to lose his grip on how he ran *his* world.

This current obsession with Sally Maguire would ease as time went on. It *was* tied in with what he'd never had with his father. She embodied the need that had never been answered—couldn't ever be answered now. But it felt good to have her. He just had to keep a reasonable perspective on the situation.

Though reason was swallowed up by a surge of desire when he saw her emerge from the house to meet and greet him. Her head was tilted towards the incoming helicopter, her hair a glorious riot of red-gold curls, lit by the setting sun. She wore a snug black top, outlining the lush thrust of her beautiful breasts, and a white skirt with a deep black border. The wind from the whirling blades wrapped the fabric around her long, shapely legs—legs that had wrapped themselves around him in uninhibited passion.

The muscles around his groin tightened. He grabbed the cooler bag containing the bottle of Veuve Clicquot, ready to alight from the helicopter as soon as it landed. He couldn't wait a second later than he had to, the need to feel her body against his again racing through his veins.

She was smiling—not the polite smile she'd put on for his first visit. This was a smile of joyous welcome, a champagne smile that shot bubbles of exhilaration through Jack's brain and put a huge grin on his face as he leapt from his seat and strode towards her.

* * *

He was so vibrantly handsome. Sally felt her whole body tingling from the rush of pleasure at seeing him again, thrilling to the eagerness in his step which surely telegraphed his desire to be with her, the smile on his face leaving no doubt as to his pleasure in seeing her, too, the bright sparkling blue of his eyes, no darkness at all because she was bringing sunshine into his life—a wild giddy thought that made her feel wonderful.

"Hi!" he said, holding up the cooler bag he carried. "I trust you have the glasses ready."

She laughed with sheer happiness at the togetherness they were about to share. "And the ice bucket," she assured him.

"Good girl!" His free arm swung around her waist and scooped her along with him as he headed for the house. "I've been looking forward to this moment all day."

"So have I." The words tripped straight off her tongue. Impossible to pretend anything else. He was hugging her close to his side, the warmth of his body lighting a glow in hers, the brush of his thighs shooting quivers of excitement right down to her toes. She loved the female feel of being physically linked to this man.

He rubbed his cheek against her hair. If she'd been a cat she would have purred. As it was, it felt as though her heart was beating in her throat. She put her arm around his waist, snuggling closer, gloatingly glad now that she'd had the foresight to ask Jeanette to prepare a dinner that could be simply heated up when they were ready for it, giving the housekeeper and her husband the evening off in their own cottage. However embarrassingly obvious it had been that she wanted to be alone with Jack no longer mattered, not with this glorious sense of anticipation buzzing through her body.

"What about your bag?" she asked, suddenly remembering Graham wasn't here to collect it from the helicopter and they had already stepped into the foyer.

"Bill will drop it off here. We'll leave the door

open for him. He'll close it as he goes," came the quick reply.

Jack didn't so much as pause in his step. Neither did she, content to be swept across the foyer, down the hall to the master suite, shutting out the outside world, sharing his urgency, revelling in it. She'd left the door to it open so he could see all the marvellous changes to the bedroom straightaway, but he made no immediate comment on the redecorating.

"Ah! Glasses on the table," he said with satisfaction, as though the rest of the room rated no attention at all, taking Sally with him as he made a beeline for the coffee table.

"Jack, do you like what's been done?" she cried, wanting to hear his approval.

He set the cooler bag down next to the ice bucket and turned to her, both arms drawing her into his embrace, his eyes blazing with an intensity that was focused entirely on her. "*You* like it so it must be right, and I don't care about anything else."

She didn't think about that statement right then, not for days afterwards. She heard the raw passion in his voice, saw naked desire burning in his eyes, and her heart was a wild thing, beating like a bongo drum, intent on driving a primitive dance to some ultimate end.

His mouth crashed down on hers with a ravaging hunger that instantly ignited a fierce need to feed it. She kissed him back with a wanton savagery that would have stunned her with disbelief in a saner moment, their tongues duelling for more and more intense sensation, teeth scraping, lips meshing in a mad need to taste everything there was to taste.

Her arms were locked around his neck, her breasts crushed to his chest, her stomach furrowed by the hard erection pressing against it. One of his hands was spread around the back of her skull, fingers entwined in her hair, tugging it to shift the position of her head as he broke from her mouth to rain hotly possessive kisses around her face, her ears, her eyelids, her temples, and she was kissing him, too, his cheek, his neck, laying claim to him, fastening on the pulse at the base of his throat as he clutched her head to hold her there, under his chin, holding her to the beat of his heart.

"I want you so badly, it can't wait," he muttered, and the vibration of his need echoed her own.

"No, it can't wait," she heard herself agree.

Then they were pulling off their clothes, helping each other get naked as fast as possible, craving the feel of flesh against flesh, the heat, the intimacy, the man-woman togetherness their bodies were demanding. And, oh, it was so good, so gloriously right. Sally stood on tiptoes to press herself more totally against the hard, hot muscularity of his maleness, wanting to melt into him. She loved this man, loved him, loved him, loved him, wanted all of him so much....

He hooked a hand under her bottom, lifted her off her feet and strode to the bed, stood her down for a moment as he hurled off the silk bedspread, the heap of decorative cushions flying away with it. He laid her on the green sheet, her head on a green pillow, and the word "Yes" hissed from his lips, and his eyes glittered exultantly as he loomed over her, and she moved her legs to make room for him, curling them around his hips as he moved into position to answer the urgent yearning driving both of them.

Her body arched in sheer ecstacy as he plunged deep inside her and the same word "Yes" tore from her throat. Her inner muscles convulsed joyously around him as he bent to kiss her again, and kept kissing her, their mouths wildly matching the thrusting that sought every possible peak of sensation they could create together, intensely possessive, incredibly exciting and finally exploding into a meltdown that left them clutching each other in a fierce embrace, holding onto the blissful oneness as their hearts gradually slowed and their bodies wallowed in relaxed contentment.

Jack carried her with him as he rolled onto his back, and he stroked her skin and her hair as she lay sprawled over him, too limp to do anything but feel the rise and fall of his chest as his breathing returned to a normal rhythm. She didn't even think. Her mind was basking in a haze of pleasure.

"Happy?" Jack eventually asked, his voice furred with his own pleasure.

"Mmmm…" It was a hum of delicious euphoria.

"I think this is champagne time."

"Mmmm…"

She had enough happy bubbles in her brain, but if he wanted to add more, she had no objection.

"You stay right here," he said, gently shifting her onto the pillow as he eased out from under her, pausing to fan the long riotous curls of her hair out around her face, smiling at the effect as he did so, his eyes twinkling satisfaction. "Don't move," he instructed, then quickly flung himself off the bed and headed for the coffee table.

She felt too languorous to move, anyway. Besides, her attention was instantly captivated by the back view of his completely unadorned physique. He looked even better without clothes, male perfection to her eyes, broad shoulders, lean hips, taut cheeky butt, strongly muscular arms and legs, though not bulging out of proportion. She imagined he worked out to keep fit but was not a gym junky, absorbed in building himself up. His smooth olive skin gleamed with good health, and she looked forward to stroking it, consciously feeling its texture when he returned to the bed.

She watched him take the bottle from the cooler bag, pop the cork with a deft efficiency that suggested he was well practised at the art. The idea that he had celebrated having sex with other women, just like this, took the lovely fizz out of the moment, but Sally quickly told herself not to let anything spoil what was good between them right now.

He filled the two glasses with the expertise of a champagne connoisseur—no overflow— propped the bottle in the ice-bucket, then turned with a glass in each hand, grinning at the sight of her waiting for him exactly where he'd placed her, lying in totally naked abandonment.

A weird little wave of self-consciousness prompted the comment, "You haven't even looked at the Monet, Jack."

It didn't draw a glance now, either. His gaze did not waver from her, his eyes drinking her in from head to foot and back again as he strolled towards the bed. "You far outshine any painting, Sally. A vibrant living work of art."

The warm appreciation in his voice, the pleasure twinkling in his eyes, instantly dispelled her unease about how she looked to him. "Can I move now?" she asked.

He laughed. "As long as it's not away from me."

"I can't drink champagne lying down."

As she hitched herself up into a sitting position, he set the filled glasses on the bedside table and piled pillows behind her. "Comfortable?" he said teasingly.

"Yes, thanks, but you've left no pillows for you."

His gaze flicked down to her breasts. "Oh, I think I can find the perfect softness for me."

Aware of her nipples stiffening into hard bullets, Sally looked down, too, then couldn't stop herself from checking out Jack's sexual equipment, remembering how wonderfully powerful it had felt inside her. Like the rest of him, perfect masculinity, she thought, and the urge to touch was too tempting to resist. She leaned over and ran her fingertips lightly over the soft velvet skin, awed that it could become so hard and strong.

"Mmm…nice," Jack murmured huskily.

"I think so," Sally said with a flirty little laugh, lifting her hand for the glass of champagne and feeling herself flush at her own boldness.

"You are beautiful, Sally Maguire." His vivid blue eyes locked onto hers as he passed her the glass. "Have I told you that?"

"No. Not until now." Did he really think so, or was it simply something he said in the grip of sexual pleasure?

"I thought you were beautiful at fourteen. You're even more so as a woman."

At fourteen? Her mind boggled at the thought he'd held that image of her all these years. It couldn't be true, yet the look in his eyes was making her *feel* beautiful, and it was a wonderful feeling.

She remembered her first impression of him— the most strikingly handsome young man she'd ever seen, the strong aura of purpose about him. "I never forgot you, Jack. You left your mark on me that day," she confessed.

"My mark…" he repeated musingly.

"I didn't know about you before you came, but then I did, and nothing was quite the same after that. So many things started to feel wrong." She shook her head ruefully. "There was nothing I could do to correct the situation but I thought about you. A lot."

He smiled, his eyes taking on a wicked glint. "I aim to keep you thinking of me, and not so much from a distance."

"You can close in any time," she invited, feeling deliciously wicked herself as she sipped her champagne and ogled him over the rim of the glass.

He laughed and sat on the edge of the bed. "I'll do that. Just you sit there and enjoy your drink while I enjoy mine."

But he didn't sip from his glass. He dipped his fingers into it and shook droplets around the tip of one of her breasts. Then he swooped down to lick up the fizzing bubbles, his tongue swirling around the tightly protruding nipple, his mouth closing over it, sucking. Sally's breath caught in her throat. Her stomach contracted as a bolt of excitement arced through it.

He repeated the action with her other breast. She didn't enjoy her drink. She forgot all about it, though her hand gripped the glass hard, as though it was an anchor to save her from being completely swept away and splintered into pieces. As it was, her body quivered uncontrollably when he trickled champagne into her navel and sipped from it.

He lifted his head and grinned at her as he moved lower down on the bed. "Drink up, my darling girl. We're supposed to be celebrating together. And if you pretend this isn't happening, it's more challenging for me, more exciting for you," he added wickedly.

She tried, gulping down her champagne as he dribbled his over the heat of her sex and lapped it up—unimaginably erotic stuff that blew her mind—the coolness, the heat, repeated over and over again, the exquisite sensitivity of his tongue stroking her most intimate femininity. It was so exciting, she could hardly bear it. Her whole body was throbbing like a volcano about to explode. It was impossible to keep pretending. Somehow she made herself wait until both their glasses had been emptied, then flung hers aside, jack-knifed up and grabbed his head.

"No more, no more," she cried, dragging him up, wild to have him inside her again. "I need you now. Now!"

"Have me then," he growled.

And it was so heavenly to feel the huge rush of him filling her need, satisfying it, and she clasped him to her with all of her being, exulting in the sheer magical pleasure of feeling so deeply connected to him. She kissed him in a frenzy of passionate possession, her hands tangling themselves in his hair, her legs wound around him, urging on the marvellous rhythm that reinforced and heightened the intensity of their union. Together they climbed climactic mountains and finally reached a state of satiation that let them drift down into a lovely sensual peace.

Eventually Jack suggested they treat themselves to a spa bath as a revival measure. They took the bottle of champagne and their glasses with them and luxuriated in the bubbling water, Sally drinking more slowly, more appreciatively this time, realising it was very expensive French champagne and delicious on the palate, almost as delicious as lazily caressing Jack's naked body with her own, floating around him, their eyes smiling their happiness in each other.

"Your next World Cup event is the Royal Easter Show in Sydney, isn't it?" he remarked, hooking his foot behind her back to bring her closer.

"Yes," she agreed, sliding forward to sit over his groin. What he'd done and said to her in the bedroom had completely banished any inhibitions about her own body, making it a joy to take any liberty with his.

He grinned at her wicked response. "You could stay with me in my apartment while you're in the city. I'll take you to the showground for your competition each day."

"I'd like that," she said, leaning forward to give him a thank-you kiss, delighted with the invitation into his world.

He turned the kiss into a far more intoxicating one. "Right now I can't have enough of you, Sally Maguire," he murmured against her mouth.

Nor she of him.

She didn't care about the "right now" part.

Spending Easter with him in Sydney sounded wonderful to her.

As long as he wanted her she was his.

She blanked her mind to any end to their relationship sometime in the future. She didn't want to think about anything but what they were sharing right now, and she didn't, not until the weekend was over and Jack had gone back to his life in the city.

Then Jane called.

And Sally, still full of her feelings for Jack Maguire, spilled them out to her sister, wanting Jane to be happy for her.

Unhappily, the response was very different.

CHAPTER ELEVEN

SHOCK…

It didn't matter how Sally explained the situation, shock came back at her in every word Jane spoke. Pained shock.

"Oh, no!"

"You didn't let him…"

"He had it planned all along."

"You fell into his trap, Sally."

"He's got you right where he wants you."

"But, Jane, please understand… I love him," Sally protested. "I've never been in love before and it's marvellous. Truly…"

"I bet he hasn't said he loves you," she returned hard and fast. "He set out to seduce you from day one. Which is why he didn't want me there whenever he visited. He wanted you and he aimed to have you, just like Mum said."

"That sounds so cold-blooded and it's not, Jane. I swear to you it's not," she pleaded. "What I'm sharing with Jack is very hot and passionate. On both sides."

Silence.

Sally sighed. "I'm sorry if I've embarrassed you, but please don't spoil it for me, Jane."

A long sigh at her end, then anxiously, "I hope you're being careful, Sally. You mustn't get pregnant. That wouldn't be good."

"I know. I'm on the pill to make sure nothing unplanned happens. Don't worry about it."

"I worry about you. I don't think this will last on his part."

"Whether it does or whether it doesn't, I'm having a brilliant time with Jack right now. And he's asked me to stay with him in Sydney when I'm competing at the Royal Easter Show. That means he isn't keeping me tucked away here on the side, like Mum said."

Another silence.

"Jane, it feels so right. Let it be. Okay?" Sally appealed with all her heart, not wanting her sister off-side with her.

"I'm frightened you'll get hurt," came the anguished reply.

"If I do, then I'll expect my nurse sister to help fix me up," she said lightly, trying to lessen the angst.

"You can always count on me, Sally. Always."

The fervent assertion was something positive to end the call on. "I know," she answered softly. "Love you, Jane. Always."

And Sally knew she would love Jack Maguire always. True love didn't get switched on and off. He might not love her, though it felt as though he did. They had a connection that went beyond sex. That had to mean something. But was it a good or bad connection in his mind? Was he getting some dark satisfaction from who she was?

She couldn't quite shake off what Jane had said. Jack had admitted he'd wanted her all along—the whole experience of her—and he'd bought time to make that happen with the year-long contract. And quite possibly the redecorating of the master suite had been aimed at seducing her.

He hadn't really cared about what had been done, except in so far as it was *right* for her—a master planner setting up the scene for a successful seduction, making her the mistress of this house in every sense—no trace of her mother left in place—a grateful little mistress who waited on him, ready to give him pleasure until he'd had enough of it.

Her heart cringed at this picture of herself. Her mind argued there had been no seduction. They'd already had sex before the redecorating had been completed. Unless the romantic dinner at Kirkton Park had been a softening-up measure, deliberately promoting the attraction she felt so she'd be willing to have more of him—a very seductive dinner with champagne and roses.

Was it only sex with Jack?

Right now I can't have enough of you.

A chilling little shiver ran down her spine as she remembered those words, spoken so hotly against her mouth.

When would he have enough?

By the end of the year?

It made her feel sick.

And that was wrong.

She was happy with him.

She wanted to stay happy with him.

I won't think that horrid dark stuff! I won't! she told herself fiercely. *I'll just take each day as it comes and love every minute I have with him.*

She took that resolution with her when she travelled down to Sydney for the Royal Easter Show, determined that nothing would spoil their time together.

She loved his penthouse apartment at Woolloomooloo with its magnificent view of Sydney Harbour, loved being with him, sharing his bed and the excitement of the show. They flew in by helicopter each day Sally was competing in events, and in her free time, they walked through the exhibition halls together, ate pink fairy floss as a laughing reminder of childhood treats, won prizes at various stalls—all great fun.

She did well in the minor showjumping events, collecting a first and a third with her second-string horses. The big one, carrying points for inclusion in the World Cup team, was on the last day, and if she won again on Midnight Magic, a blue ribbon would truly cap this trip to Sydney.

The top-class event was scheduled for mid-afternoon. Sally had a light lunch with Jack, who then left her with Tim to oversee Midnight Magic's preparation and get her mind focused on leading her horse to perform perfectly. Jack would be watching them from the grandstand with the best vantage point for viewing the showjumping. She knew where his seat was, knew he would be willing her to win. She was riding a high, and hoped it would go even higher.

* * *

"Jack Maguire?"

The sharp call of his name jerked his attention away from the main ring where Sally would soon be competing. He frowned at the aggressive tone, not recognising the voice, and was surprised to see it had come from Sally's younger sister, the mouse-like Jane, who was making her away along the row of seats towards him.

Sally had made no mention of her sister coming to watch. Probably an impulse thing on Jane's part. She didn't look pleased to see him here. In fact, she looked distinctly angry, her hands clenched in fighting mode, her slender body stiff with tension, her brown eyes not shying away from him today. They were blazing with the intent to confront.

"Jane," he said, rising to his feet and acknowledging her with a nod, curious about her reaction to seeing him and what was behind it. He gestured to the seat he'd bought for Sally to watch other events—vacant while she was competing. "Would you like to join me?"

"Thank you, I would," she replied with gritty determination. "I have quite a bit to say to you."

She certainly had the bit between the teeth, Jack thought, plonking herself in the seat beside his and barely waiting for him to resume his before breaking into an impassioned speech, her eyes hotly accusing.

"Sally never did anything bad to you. She's never done anything bad to anyone. And it's terribly, terribly wrong of you to take her down over some dark sense of injustice to you."

Take her down? This was nonsense. He'd set Sally up with everything she wanted. And Jane was benefiting from it, as well. She certainly wasn't acting like a victim today.

"It wasn't Sally's fault that your father adopted her and gave her what you were more entitled to have," she raved on. "It wasn't her fault that our mother kept you an outcast. To make her pay for your pain is just…just wicked."

She was so incensed she spluttered into momentary speechlessness, giving Jack the chance to get an incisive word in. "Sally is *not* paying for anything."

"I don't mean money!" she exploded again. "I bet the money you've laid out isn't even a dent in your billions. It's what you're doing with it… with Sally…that's so evil."

"Evil?" Jack's patience was sharply pricked. "What the hell are you on about?"

"You…leading my sister to hell," came the punchy retort. "She's fallen blindly in love with you…"

In lust, Jack mentally corrected. Sally enjoyed the fantastic sex they had as much as he did. He'd led her to heaven, not hell.

"…but I'm not blinded by you, Jack Maguire. You're using her to satisfy some rotten hole in your heart, and when you've got all you wanted from her, you'll abandon her, just as you've abandoned every other woman in your life, once the steam has run out of the sex."

That touched a nerve. "What do you know about my life?" he snapped.

"I researched you," she flung back at him. "When Sally told me where you were with her, I looked up your social life in the newspaper archives. That's some record you've got. A stream of beautiful women led up your garden path but none of them able to hang on to you. And Sally won't be any different, will she?"

"Sally *is* different!" he grated, his jaw clenching in anger at the affront of this snip of a girl, digging into his life.

"She's different all right. Different because she isn't some hardened sophisticate. She'll be devastated when you walk away. But you don't care about that, do you? You will have played your vengeful little game, fed your dark side with who she is…"

"That's enough!" he cut in, barely containing the anger she'd stirred. His hand sliced a denial as he hurled a few truths back at her. "You use society tattle to sit in judgement of me? You don't have a clue where I'm at, Jane Maguire. Why don't you try trusting your sister's judgement of me instead of stirring up a nest of snakes?"

"I saw you in action at the solicitor's office. You're hard and you're ruthless," she hurled straight back at him. "All the years of our growing up together…Sally was always the one to protect me when there was trouble, taking the brunt of any punishment. It's not fair you picked on her." She shook her head in anguish. "Not fair! If you have any decency at all, you should let her off the hook before it goes too deep."

Understanding suddenly sliced through Jack's outrage. The mouse had steeled herself to become a lion, wanting to protect the sister who had always protected her. She was blundering into completely alien territory, driven by sisterly love which was demanding action from her. However off-line she was, Jack found himself respecting the urge that had brought her to face him with her desperate misgivings about his motivations.

In truth, he had to admit she wasn't so far off-line. His bitterly frustrating non-relationship with his father was a factor in what he'd set up with Sally. But *punishing* her for what his father and Lady Ellen had done to him played no part in it. And deliberately hurting her was so far from his mind…

"You're in a position to have so much else," Jane pleaded. "It wouldn't hurt you to let Sally go."

He was having the best time of his life. No way was he about to walk away from it. Besides, whenever this passion for all that Sally was did eventually burn out, he'd never just *abandon* her. One way or another, he'd take care of her needs. He wasn't like his father.

"You don't know what you're talking about, Jane," he said tersely. "You're assuming stuff that isn't true."

"Tell me what isn't true," she challenged, not believing him. "Of everything I've said, tell me what isn't true. Give me a slice of honesty."

"I did not force anything on Sally. She chose."

"Huh!" It was a derisive snort. "A choice loaded with heavy persuasives."

True. But from what he knew of Sally's character, nothing would have persuaded her to go to bed with him if she hadn't wanted to. "You should know your sister better."

"I've never known her like this. She's always been so sensible, so strong in working things through. You've messed her up, Jack Maguire, for your own vindictive, selfish satisfaction. And don't tell me you didn't set out to do it, because you did. Demanding I stay away whenever you visited, ensuring you had a clear run at her."

That was true, too.

"I'm not breaking Sally's contract with you by coming here," she pointed out. "This isn't your property. You can't order me to leave and I won't until I make you give up this...this black vendetta."

He shook his head over her self-imposed mission. She'd asked for a slice of honesty and he gave it to her. "The past does colour what I feel with Sally. It colours what she feels with me, too. You can't…"

"What *do* you feel?" she retorted, aiming straight at his heart.

Be damned if he was going to lay himself open to any more criticism! "That's not your business. It's between me and Sally."

"She's my sister. I'm her family. I care. And I have every right to question if you care."

"Sally Maguire…riding Midnight Magic."

The announcement, boomed from loudspeakers, ripped Jack's attention away from Jane. He'd missed the previous riders, didn't know what Sally was competing against. She was already in the ring, walking her horse to the starting line, her head lifted towards the grandstand, looking for his encouragement and support.

Any moment now she'd spot him, see her sister sitting right next to him—her sister who had undoubtedly poured out to Sally the same hostile suspicions she'd just loaded on him—and the whole tenor of this confrontation told him Jane had not told Sally what she intended to do.

Seeing them together might upset her, might become a major distraction from what *she* had to do to get Midnight Magic jumping smoothly. And the jumps for the World Cup competition were formidably high. If she lost her concentration…

Jack grabbed Jane's hand and surged up from his seat, dragging Jane with him, raising their linked hands high above their heads for Sally to see.

"Smile at your sister," he commanded. "Pretend you've made peace with me. She mustn't feel tense about us when she's about to take on those jumps."

Sally saw them. Her shoulders stiffened. Jack knew a jolt of shock was running through her. He shot a quick glance at Jane who looked gobsmacked by the action he'd forced.

"Smile, damn you! This is Sally's big number. It's important to her."

She belatedly stretched her mouth into a smile. Jack beamed a wide grin. "Now clap your hands above your head to show you're madly urging her on to do her best. And keep smiling."

He released her hand to do the same himself and felt an intense wave of relief when Jane copied the wild applause. Sally smiled. She was relaxing. He fiercely hoped she could put them out of her mind now, or at least know they were in harmony on one point—wanting her to perform well.

"Sit down in front," a man behind them bellowed.

Deciding that nothing more could be done to fix the situation, Jack sat down.

Jane slowly sank onto the seat beside him. "You *do* care," she said, as though stunned by the fact.

"Yes, I care," he slung at her with dark ferocity, still worried about the effect her meeting with him might have on Sally. "And if you care, you'll shut up and let me concentrate on willing your sister to take her horse cleanly over every jump."

The starter gun went off.

Jane didn't say another word.

Jack totally ignored her presence, his whole being tied to Sally and the horse she was riding, every muscle in his body instinctively lifting as they lifted, relaxing as each jump was cleared, tensing at the approach of the next one. Midnight Magic was a big horse. If Sally's control of it wasn't spot on, if it caught a leg on one of the rails, if it fell...

The relief when they'd safely completed the course was huge. He hadn't even looked at the clock, had no idea if their time was competitive, if they had a chance of winning. He was happy that they'd made it through without a falter, neither horse nor rider hurt by a mistake.

Again he was on his feet, clapping madly.

Jane joined him.

Sally smiled and waved at them as she made her exit from the ring.

"She's happy," he said with satisfaction, then turned to her sister as they resumed their seats, knowing that peace between them had to be established for Sally to remain happy. "I'm sorry for shutting you out. It was wrong of me. On many counts," he added wryly, well remembering his own deep resentment at being treated as an outcast. "You've shown me today you are truly Sally's family, Jane, standing up for her, caring… It's not something that's been in my life since my mother died. I didn't fully appreciate the bond the two of you have."

She stared at him as though he had grown two heads and she was confused over which one she should believe in.

Jack pressed for a stay of judgement. "When this event is over—" he nodded towards the ring "—I think Sally would be pleased if we both go down to congratulate her on a great ride. Is that okay with you?"

"Yes," she said dazedly.

Intent on removing any sense of conflict between them, he suggested, "Perhaps you'd like to accompany us to a celebratory dinner afterwards. Make it a happy family Easter."

She swallowed hard. Her brown eyes filled with agitated appeal. "I'm sorry if I got it wrong. I was just so worried…"

"Let's move on, Jane," he cut in quickly, firmly. "That's what I'm doing with Sally. Moving on to something better. Will you try it with me?"

He watched the lion metamorphose back into the mouse, the brown eyes flickering with apprehension, hands picking at each other. "You won't tell Sally what I said to you?" she begged anxiously. "She wouldn't like it that I…"

Jack reached out and gave her nervous hands a reassuring squeeze. "You were very brave on her behalf. I'll always remember that, Jane, but the rest is forgotten. Okay?"

She heaved a sigh of relief and gave him a shaky little smile. "You're a very forceful man, Jack Maguire. I guess I can only hope it will be okay."

"So many things shape our lives, our choices, our decisions, but in the end we make our own destiny," he said with the strength of his own inner conviction. "In one sense, our father brought the three of us to this moment, but what we make of it…that's up to us."

She searched his eyes, still anxious about his intentions, then slowly nodded. "I'd like to have dinner with you and Sally. I'd like to get to know you."

"Good!" He smiled to show there were no hard feelings on his side. "Now let's watch the rest of Sally's competition."

He turned his gaze to the ring where another rider was about to start the course, but he didn't give his full attention to watching. His mind kept circling around what he'd just accomplished with Jane, the hurdles *he* had jumped to get the outcome he wanted—no clouds threatening to blot out the sunshine of his relationship with Sally.

Family ties…

He was becoming more involved than he'd meant to be.

Where was he going with this?

As long as it felt good, ride with it, he told himself.

It was okay for Jane to be on the sideline.

Sally was the main event.

CHAPTER TWELVE

Seven Months Later

THE Melbourne Cup—the horse race that routinely stopped a nation on the first Tuesday in November—virtually commanded the attention of everyone in Australia for the three minutes it took to run.

The roses at Flemington Racecourse were in full bloom. The weather was kind—a bright, sunny day. The crowd was wonderfully colourful. People in mad costumes and wild hats made a fun contrast to the serious contenders for the fashions in the field prize, all of whom were seriously dressed to the nines in their designer clothes.

Sally and Jack were guests in the sheikhs' marquee which was packed with A-list celebrities, indulging themselves with the endless supply of fine wines and gourmet food. A beautician and a milliner were also on hand to fix up any little mishap to a lady's appearance. Nothing was allowed to spoil anyone's day in this marquee. Utter luxury abounded—a beautiful place made for the beautiful people, of which Sally was one with Jack Maguire as her escort.

During the year, she had attended other race meetings with Jack, at Royal Randwick and at Rosehill Gardens in Sydney. He owned a string of racehorses, including those taken over from his father, and took a keen interest in their performance, especially on the big prize days. Sally enjoyed the carnival atmosphere, loved watching the horses racing and was always happy to be with Jack.

They had become an established couple at these outings, and the speculative gossip their appearance together had initially raised was no longer a hot item on anyone's lips. The two of them being publicly linked didn't stop other women from vying for Jack's attention, but they were invariably disappointed in their efforts to detach him from Sally. It made her feel they had a solid relationship, though Jack never spoke of marriage, never seemed to look to the future except for deciding on the next time he could be with her. He'd never said he loved her, either. For the most part, he lived his life in Sydney and she lived hers at Yarramalong.

All too often she wished for more of him. Then she told herself that what they had together was great and she was lucky to have what he gave of himself. She couldn't imagine being with any other man, anyway. Even Jane had come around to accepting them as a couple, though she occasionally muttered it was too much a one-sided relationship with Sally always being there for him—virtually on call—while he just fitted her into his life when it suited him.

True enough, but to Sally's mind, there was no point in arguing over the arrangement. Jack had spelled out the terms of any relationship with him right at the beginning and she had accepted them. If there was to be a change, it had to come from him.

She would have to speak to him soon about the future of the property, though. The contracted year of her management would be over in another ten weeks. She had to know what would happen then, not only to settle her own sense of insecurity but that of the staff, as well.

Today, however, was too festive a day to be worrying about things she had no control over. It was fun watching all the people on parade, discussing with Jack and the other guests what horses might have the best chance of winning, eating oysters, drinking champagne, feeling great in the very stylish black-and-white outfit she'd bought for this event.

She was having a brilliant time until her mother entered the marquee on the arm of her new billionaire husband, Clifford Byrne, a seventy-two-year-old New Zealander whom she'd recently married in Las Vegas, a quickie wedding with no family invited on either side, which had undoubtedly suited Sir Leonard Maguire's widow, not having to produce her own children nor face any criticism from his— a fait accompli.

They both looked very pleased with themselves, the showcase wife decked out in new diamonds and a beautiful wheat-coloured ensemble, the rather elderly gentleman in a formal morning suit and top hat, beaming with his new lease on life. Sally heartily wished they had graced some other marquee with their presence.

Her nerves were instantly on edge. Once her mother spotted Jack, she wouldn't be able to resist flouting her victory over the bankruptcy he'd meant her to suffer. And seeing her disloyal daughter at his side…she was bound to make something nasty of that, too.

As it turned out, she did not confront Jack, waiting until he left Sally's side to place some bets at the TAB desk before making her move. Having whispered something to her husband, who immediately gave her an indulgent smile and a nod of assent, she slid away from him and made a beeline for Sally, bestowing fleeting smiles of acknowledgement to the party guests who called for her attention, not pausing to engage in conversation.

The eyes she trained on Sally were glittering with malicious purpose. This was not going to be a forgive-all, make peace, let bygones be bygones meeting, though neither of her adopted daughters had made any bad waves for her this past year and there was no reason for her to be vicious now, particularly since she'd managed to re-feather her bed with such spectacular success. Sally steeled herself to be gracious, hoping that might deflect whatever nastiness was on her mother's mind.

"Good to see you looking so splendid, Mother," she said before an opening salvo was shot at her. "And congratulations on your marriage. It obviously suits you very well."

"Yes." She visibly preened. "And I've made sure

I won't be left destitute this time. I got Clifford to give me a marriage settlement up front."

Hardly "destitute" last time, Sally thought.

"Much more than a piddling one hundred thousand dollars a year," she added with pointed mockery. "Which will very shortly end for you, you stupid girl."

A hot rush of blood instantly scorched Sally's cheeks at the reference to her contract with Jack. More than three-quarters of the stipulated year had gone.

"And don't tell me Jack Maguire isn't getting what he paid for," her mother ran on, expressing her contempt for the situation her daughter had accepted. "You've even given him the satisfaction of flaunting the fact in public that you're his callgirl and nothing more, coming here to the Melbourne Cup on his arm."

"It's not like that," Sally protested, though it was in a way, enough to make her feel horribly belittled.

She was subjected to a blast of derision.

"You've been putty in his hands from the start, without enough sense to turn his game to your advantage. Blackjack Maguire wins again and you're the big loser, Sally. He'll hammer that home very shortly unless you take my advice and get yourself pregnant to him. There's still time for you to play that trump card."

"No." Sally shook her head, vehemently negating the suggestion. "I won't."

"Then you'll end up with nothing when he kicks you out at the end of the year," her mother jeered.

"You don't know him," Sally fiercely retaliated. "Jack won't do that."

One eyebrow arched in sceptical challenge. "Has he given his word that he won't?"

"We haven't talked about it."

The admission provoked an ugly laugh. "Don't want to know. Hiding your head in the sand. You are such a patsy. He's sucked you in and he'll spit you out."

Sally's jaw clenched. She hated the spin her mother was putting on the situation and saying anything more would only feed the nastiness, prolonging it. Besides, she didn't believe—wouldn't believe—Jack was the callous monster her mother was making him out to be. She glared back her disbelief, which seemed to amuse her mother even more.

"Remember Leonard's solicitor, Victor Newell?" she drawled provocatively. "He now handles all my legal business. As well as Jack Maguire's."

Sally frowned over the reference to the man who had drawn up her contract with Jack. Surely all his clients' legal business carried a confidentiality that forbade discussion of them to anyone else. She didn't understand the point of the connection her mother was making.

"I was in Victor's office only last week, and what should I see on his secretary's desk?"

The pause was loaded with malicious triumph.

Sally gritted her teeth even harder, refusing to bite.

"The title deeds of the property at Yarramalong,"

her mother rolled out with the glee of lighting a fuse that was bound to lead to a destructive conclusion. "Now why do you suppose those deeds would need current attention? Could it be that Blackjack Maguire has a buyer for the property and he's about to transfer ownership, I asked myself?"

Sally felt the hot blood that had rushed to her face earlier drain from it just as fast, leaving her skin cold and clammy. It couldn't be true. Jack wouldn't sell off her home without telling her, would he?

"So I inquired of Victor if the property was on the market, pretending an interest in buying it," her mother went on merrily.

Sally's heart stopped. Her lungs suspended all activity. Her very life was hanging on the answer.

"'Not to my knowledge,' Victor said, but his eyes flickered evasively and I knew something was going down. No doubt a private deal. As private as the bankruptcy rescue Jack Maguire perpetrated on Leonard. All done behind doors so that devious bastard can deliver the coup de grace with maximum shock. As he did to me." She leaned forward, her eyes boring into Sally's as she venomously added, "And will do to you when your time is up."

"No!" The word exploded from her lips as the breath she'd held was finally expelled from her chest.

"Yessss," her mother hissed back at her. "Unless you do something to win."

The goad was in her voice, in the stabbing intensity of her eyes, and Sally mentally reeled back from it. She would not live her mother's way. Never! No matter what Jack did or didn't do. Maybe she'd been living in a fool's paradise, but she'd rather be a fool than a snaky gold-digger.

"This is all speculation. Your kind of speculation, Mother," she grated out, denying it any weight.

The repudiation earned a mountain of disgust. "Then stay blind, you idiot child! If the truth

hurts you, it's a hurt well deserved for not listening to me."

Her eyes raked Sally with blistering scorn.

"Lady Ellen…"

Jack's voice, cold and challenging… Jack
stepping up to Sally's side, giving her the comfort
of his support, his arm sliding around hers, deliberately hooking them together. *Flaunting* their
relationship in front of her mother? Winner of everything he'd set out to take? Sally stiffened,
unable to shake off the barbs that were dripping
their poison into her mind.

Lady Ellen disdained any reply to the man who
had wreaked his vengeance on her. With a haughty
toss of her beautifully styled and coloured blond
hair, she turned her back on both of them and
headed off to her trophy husband, who provided
all the evidence needed that *she* was a winner,
despite her stepson's plotting to make her a loser.

"What was that all about?" Jack demanded in
a taut voice, probably aware of her tension and
not liking it.

Sally forced herself to turn and look straight into the face of the man she had loved so unreservedly. His sharp blue eyes scanned hers with laser-like intensity, wanting to pinpoint whatever problem needed fixing. Did he really care about her, or was he simply ruthlessly intent on maintaining the status quo until he was ready to end it?

"Am I your callgirl, Jack?" she asked searchingly. "Is that how you think of me?"

"No!" The denial was instant and strongly voiced. His brows lowered into a dark frown. Anger flashed from his eyes. "Is that your mother's interpretation of our relationship?"

No more head in the sand. "I'd like you to give me yours," she insisted unflinchingly.

"You can scrub out *callgirl* for a start," he answered tersely. "Not once have I ever thought of you as taking that role in my life."

"Yet I have, haven't I?" she said wryly. "You call and I do whatever you want."

"Because *you* want to," he retorted with conviction, though for a moment the conviction wavered. "You do know you're not obliged to please me? I never pressed you to, beyond putting out the welcome mat whenever I visit the property, which was part of our contract."

"No. You didn't press me. It's been my choice to have you as my lover." Perhaps a blind choice, a foolish choice, but hers nonetheless.

"And you've been happy with me," he pushed.

"Yes."

"Then don't let that bitch erode what we have together," he said forcefully.

"What do we have, Jack?" Her eyes pleaded for the absolute truth. "I know you warned me not to expect a relationship with you to last a long time, but I did think I'd sense when you were losing interest."

"I haven't lost interest," he declared without hesitation. "Why would you even think it?"

She shook her head. There was no denying the desire she felt pouring from him—the same physical desire he drew from her. It couldn't be deception on his part. The sexual connection they shared was a natural force and it hadn't been diminished by the familiarity of being together all these months.

Just last night it had been as white-hot as ever, and her body was reacting to it right now, her heart pounding, her stomach contracting, little quivers of excitement running down her thighs. Nevertheless, she couldn't quite wipe out the doubts her mother had so insidiously planted in her mind.

"Why would Victor Newell be looking at the title deeds to the property, Jack?"

It jolted him. The blast of desire for her receded, swiftly overtaken by narrow-eyed calculation, chilling the heat he'd generated a moment ago.

"Are you in the process of selling it?" she asked point-blank, and in her anxiety to get the truth, quickly added, "My mother saw the file on his secretary's desk, which suggested some current business was in hand."

"I see," he muttered, his mouth thinning into a grim line.

Fear stabbed at Sally's heart. Was her mother right? "We haven't talked about the future, Jack. I…" She swallowed hard, trying to reduce the thickening lump in her throat. "I trusted the…the sense that you were satisfied with… with our arrangement."

"More than satisfied," he slung at her vehemently, his gaze slicing around the crowd of guests, intent on finding the source of threat to his pleasure. Anger pulsed from him. When he spotted her mother, re-attached to Clifford Byrne, his whole demeanour changed, as though he was bracing himself to go into battle—a battle he relished. "Come…" His hand gripped hers, fingers inter-lacing with iron-fist strength. "We will address these concerns to the woman who raised them."

He set out, pulling Sally after him. Her whole being recoiled from confronting her mother, memories of how abusive she could be flooding her mind, throwing her into fearful agitation. "Jack, please…I don't want a scene. I just want to know…"

"Don't worry!" His eyes flashed derisive confidence. "Lady Ellen is not about to show her true colours in front of Clifford Byrne."

"But this is between us. It's not her business."

"She made it her business."

"Oh, please…let it go, Jack."

He paused, scooping her into his embrace, holding her tight as he fiercely replied, "Let it go that she made you feel bad? Let it go that she painted me as a man with no honour or integrity? Oh no, my darling girl! Her poison has to be scotched before her success with you encourages her to spread it. She's put your reputation and mine on the line and I will not let her tarnish them."

"I'm sorry!" Sally cried, wishing she hadn't let her mother get to her. "I do believe you have honour and integrity, Jack. It's just that you told me I can't count on any future with you and I didn't want to bring it up, so when she hit me with the title deeds of the property— I realise you have every right to sell it if you want to—"

He placed a finger over her lips to stop the wild gabbling. His eyes blazed into hers, intent on searing away any doubt whatsoever. "I'm *not* selling. And neither have you been selling your body to me. I know that in my bones, Sally. In my bones. And I will not have that mean-hearted witch of a woman labelling you my callgirl. Come with me now and trust me to deal with it. Okay?"

She nodded, too choked up to speak, and re-alising nothing was going to deter him anyway. Hard, ruthless purpose was driving him. Memories of how he had dealt with her mother at her father's funeral, and at the reading of the will, crowded her mind—a dangerous man who held all the cards and played them with master-ful force, relentless in his determination to balance the scales. Yet what cards would he play this time to beat her mother's game?

Trust me...

Sally clung to those words, fighting back the fear of being publicly humiliated by her mother. She had trusted Jack. She wanted to keep trusting him. She had to. Or everything she'd done was wrong.

The group of people chatting with Clifford Byrne and her mother automatically made room for Jack to insert himself and Sally. No one shut him out these days. In fact, his powerful presence instantly galvanised their attention. No-one was going to drift away from this scene, either. They'd hang on every word and inevitably repeat it later. A terrible tension gripped Sally. She desperately hoped Jack could make this turn out right.

"Mr. Byrne, I'm Jack Maguire, Lady Ellen's stepson. And I don't think you've had the pleasure of meeting her daughter, Sally."

The surprise introduction flummoxed the New Zealander into taking the offered hand and smiling a polite delight at Sally. "Indeed, a

pleasure. We're still on our honeymoon," he said
in excuse for the oversight of not having met his
new wife's family before. "Just starting to catch
up with people, aren't we, darling?" He glanced
at his wife for her response.

She was staring at Jack, a Medusa-like stare,
undoubtedly wishing he would turn to stone.

Jack smiled at her—the smile of a tiger having
cornered his quarry—but he addressed his
words to Clifford Byrne, man to man. "Lady
Ellen caught up with Sally a few minutes ago.
I understand she was concerned for her future,
labouring under the impression I was about to
sell the property where Sally trains her horses.
I didn't want to leave Lady Ellen worried about
it at such a happy time for both of you."

"No, no, I don't want my wife worried about
anything." The doting husband patted the hand
that was hanging on his arm.

"Agreed," Jack said in the same tone of indul-
gence. "A pity Lady Ellen spotted the title deeds
file at her solicitor's office. I was keeping the

transference of the property into Sally's name as a surprise gift for her on Christmas Day, but better to have my intention out in the open now."

"*My* name?" Sally gasped in shock.

"*You* will be the new owner," Jack confirmed, turning a brilliant smile to her.

She was totally dazzled.

"Ah! Very generous of you," Clifford Byrne said approvingly.

"And I'm sure a welcome surprise to Sally," her mother said with acid-edged saccharine. "Indeed, a very generous mark of appreciation for all she's done for the property."

A sly hit at sexual favours given.

For one heart-sinking moment Sally wondered if giving her the home she'd always known was a kiss-off gift. Had Jack been this generous with all his women? But he wasn't finished with her. He cared about her feelings, cared about her future, ensuring, with the transfer of ownership of the property, that her life there could go on as long as she wanted it to. Though it was such a huge gift. Was it right to accept it if he didn't mean to share it with her?

"What she's done for me, too," Jack said warmly. "You see, Lady Ellen, having Sally in my life more than makes up for being an outcast in the past. I want to thank you for adopting her into the family. Otherwise our paths might never have crossed and I would have missed out on sharing a future with her."

The miserable turmoil lifted from Sally's heart.

He did mean to share it.

"What future do you have in mind?" her mother asked somewhat archly, putting him on the spot, probably hoping for an answer she could turn into an embarrassing scandal.

"Well, at the moment, Sally is concentrating most of her time and energy on working up to competing in the World Cup. She's made it to the team," Jack rolled out, giving her a hug and a look of pride in her achievement so far. His vivid blue eyes held hers, boring straight into her heart as he added, "Once that's over, I'm hoping she'll give some thought to marrying me and starting a family of our own."

Marriage? Children? Shock and caution quivered through a burst of hope and happiness. Was he just saying it to defeat her mother's malice?

"Good man!" Clifford Byrne cheerfully approved, reaching out to shake Jack's hand again. Which he did. Before turning a benign face to his wife. "That takes care of everything, darling. No worries."

Sally had no doubt her mother hated this resolution to the situation, but any control over it had been completely taken out of her hands. Jack had made a public declaration that couldn't be undermined. The only way it could be changed was if he changed it himself.

"Congratulations! To both of you," her mother said with a thin smile. "I hope you have a very happy future."

"Thank you," Jack replied, his tone smacking of deep satisfaction at having wrung this public well-wishing from her mother. "You, too, Lady Ellen, Mr. Byrne."

"We must make plans for another meeting," Clifford Byrne threw in, obviously feeling impelled to be hospitable to his wife's family now that they'd made themselves known to him. "Why don't you and Sally visit us in New Zealand?"

"Not in a million years," her mother bit out, the fury she'd been hiding seething through the words.

Her sucked-in husband was startled into leaning forward to look at her. "What? What's that you say?"

She glared at him, the intensity of her hatred for Jack turning the plastic beauty of her face quite ugly, the stunning force of her feeling causing Clifford Byrne to reel back, shocked by a side of her he hadn't seen before, perhaps even beginning to wonder if he had been deceived in other things by the woman he'd so hastily married.

"I believe Lady Ellen said, 'Not in a million years,'" Jack repeated with relish, delighted that she had been unmasked enough for her true colours to show. "A sentiment I happen to share," he tossed at her with a flick of contempt. "Now, if you'll excuse us, I have a horse running in the next race, and Sally and I want to watch it win."

Game over!

The poker champion had once more played a winning hand.

But had its substance been a bluff?

Or was everything he'd said real?

Sally's head was swimming with these critical questions as he led her away.

CHAPTER THIRTEEN

"ALL fixed," Jack murmured with triumphant satisfaction, steering Sally out of the marquee, heading towards the racetrack.

A huge sigh shuddered from her chest. She braved a glance at him, needing to know how much of *the fix* was fiction designed to drown her mother's attempt to muddy the waters between them. He looked happy and devilishly handsome, his eyes sparkling with unholy pleasure in the outcome he had forced.

"Are you really putting the property in my name?" she blurted out.

He laughed. "Yes, my darling girl, I am. Victor Newell is currently in the process of making it legal."

*My darling girl...*it was his pet name for her, mostly used after they made love. She'd thought it carried a deep affection for her, but she wasn't sure if it wasn't simply an expression of his pleasure in the pleasure she'd given him, the sense of intimate possession which was naturally felt at such a time. Yet this was the second time today he'd said it outside of that sexual context and it fed her burgeoning hope for the love she craved from him—a lasting love.

His mouth twisted ruefully. "I had planned to surprise you with the title deeds for Christmas, but now the secret's out, I'll have to add something else."

"No, you won't," she said anxiously. "As it is, I can't possibly match such a huge gift, and I don't think I should accept it, Jack."

"You've more than matched it, Sally. Just by being you and giving me so much of yourself."

The low sexy throb in his voice and the simmering heat in his eyes made her duck her head, using the brim of her hat to hide her face and the anguished doubt in her mind.

Was it only sex?

She could not bear the uncertainty.

"Did you mean the bit about wanting to marry me and having a family?"

She rushed out the words on a single painful breath, keeping her head lowered, frightened of giving away her feelings if he laughed it off as a ploy to ruin her mother's day.

He halted, swinging her around to face him, his arms drawing her into his embrace, his powerful thighs propping up her trembling legs, his hands pressing into the curve of her back, making her breasts push against the strong wall of his chest, forcing her to be acutely aware of the physical attraction she could not deny.

"Look at me, Sally!" he commanded.

Tears welled up in her eyes. It meant so much to her and she couldn't hide it.

"Look at me!" he repeated with urgent intensity.

* * *

Jack didn't care about the crowd of spectators jostling around them, seeking the best position to watch the race. He didn't care whether his horse won or lost. Everything but Sally was totally meaningless to him—this once-beautiful girl, whose life with their father he'd resented, this now-beautiful and wonderful woman he counted as the best thing that had ever happened to him.

Slowly, slowly, she lifted her head. Moisture clung to her eyelashes. Her eyes were wet but she did not flinch from looking straight at him. Brave Sally, determined on knowing her fate with him. He'd admired her strong spirit all along, and her vulnerability right now smote his heart. He'd played this all wrong, letting her mother's spite propel him into expressing what should have been said first to her.

He reached up and gently brushed the streak of tears from her cheeks. "I love you, Sally," he said, finally acknowledging and speaking the truth of what he felt for her. "I wasn't going to bring up marriage until after the

World Cup. I was happy to ride along with what we have, let you achieve your showjumping ambition before putting other plans for the future to you."

Her eyes widened into lovely green pools of wonder. "You…" Her throat moved convulsively. "You…love me?"

"To almost constant distraction," he admitted a touch ruefully. "When I'm not with you, I'm looking forward to how it will be when I am. There's no way I could ever let you go. You're in my blood, in my mind, in my heart. When I said love and marriage weren't on my agenda, I didn't believe any woman could make me feel that life without her was unthinkable, but you—" he ran a featherlight finger over her trembling lips "—you're the embodiment of dreams I gave up on a long time ago. In every sense."

"Oh, Jack!" Her eyes shone with a starburst of happiness. "I love you, too. So much. So very much."

She flung her arms around his neck and kissed

him, her fervent passion instantly stirring a fierce wave of possessiveness—*his* woman, now and forever—and he kissed her back, revelling in the reality of having her, holding her, loving her and being loved by her.

The loud cheering of the Melbourne Cup crowd intruded on the sweet moment. "Your horse!" Sally gasped, her mouth breaking from his.

"Never mind my horse," Jack said with a carefree laugh. "I take it you will marry me when the time is right?"

"Yes." She laughed and kissed him again, exuberant little kisses punctuated by, "Yes…yes…yes."

"Then I think we should slip off tomorrow morning and buy you an engagement ring so you can flaunt it in front of everyone for the rest of Melbourne Cup Week. A very serious engagement ring so no one will have any doubt about where you stand with me. Not even your mother will be able to overlook it."

She sighed, her mouth twisting into an ironic

grimace. "She never really cared about me and Jane. We were her insurance policy, aimed at getting a big financial settlement if my father ever deserted her for another woman."

"Forget her, Sally. She's not worth another thought."

"Can you forget her and what she did to you?"

"That page has been turned, and I'm not going to look back at it. The pages we turn together will fill my life from now on."

"Mine, too," she promised, shrugging off the brief cloud and giving him her sunshine smile. "So let's enjoy the rest of the day." Her eyes sparkled like clear water on a brilliant day. "We'll go find out if your horse won."

He laughed, hooking her arm around his to hold her close as they wove their way through the milling crowd to the winner's circle. It didn't matter where his horse had come in the race. Jack had never felt more of a winner than he did today.

Christmas

It was so different to last Christmas, Sally thought happily, no precise formality about anything, just calling out to each other to get moving and gather in the lounge room to share the gift-giving. Jack insisted on serving them a cocktail of orange juice and champagne first. Jane was completely relaxed, not anxious over pleasing her father with what she'd bought for him, not fearful of earning her mother's displeasure by acting nervously or making the wrong response to what she was given.

The tree in front of the fireplace was not decorated with a mass of pristine white and silver ornaments. It sparkled with every colour she and Jane had been able to buy, and they'd had wonderful fun decorating it together. Jack had declared it the best Christmas tree he'd ever seen—a really personal tree, obviously dressed with love and joy and a far cry from the sort of showpiece that had always left him cold.

It was not cold this morning. The midsummer sun was already hot and instead of appropriate

Christmas clothes, Jack wore only a pair of shorts, and she and Jane had donned bikinis and sarongs, ready for a swim after breakfast. Jeanette was bustling around in the kitchen, determined on giving them the most festive meals she could create, so pleased and grateful that none of them had to move from what had been their home for so long. To Jeanette and Graham and Tim, Jack was Santa Claus.

Though Jane suddenly claimed the position. "Since we don't have to do it Mum's way this year, I'm going to be Santa Claus and give out the presents," she declared, dancing over to the tree with a gleeful anticipation Sally had never before seen in her sister.

Jane had grown in confidence this year. Maybe having become a fully qualified nurse had contributed to the change in her, though her emancipation from critical parents was undoubtedly a factor in her growth as a person in her own right. Whatever…she wasn't scared of putting herself forward anymore.

"You, first, Sally."

The gift she presented was from herself. Jane had always been into crafts, a hobby she could indulge in her own room, bothering no-one. Sally hadn't even known she'd taken up scrapbooking, so it was with amazed delight she opened the gift album and saw photographs of herself on all the horses she had loved from age five upwards, each one surrounded with artistic decoration and annotated with amusing comments.

"Jane, this is marvellous! It must have taken you ages to do."

"A labour of love." Her eyes glowed with pleasure in Sally's delight. "You've been the best sister in the world to me. This was something I could do for you."

"Thank you so much!"

"Let me see," Jack said eagerly, shifting closer to Sally on the sofa so he could share the pictorial view of the little girl who started riding a pony and grew up to become a champion showjumper.

"I've got something special for you, too, Jack." Jane dashed back to the tree to fetch the next gift and returned to offer it, her confidence suddenly tottering into her old wary shyness. "At least, I hope you'll think it's special."

"If it's anywhere near as creative as what you've given Sally, I'm going to love it," he warmly assured her.

She handed him a soft parcel and stood fidgeting nervously as Jack tore off the Christmas wrapping to reveal a pure wool, hand-knitted long-sleeved jumper in royal blue. Woven into the front of it was a black horse in full leap.

"I enlarged a photo of Midnight Magic and traced it onto graph paper so I could get the stitches right," Jane quickly explained. "It will be cold over there in England for the World Cup and I thought you could wear this jumper when you're watching Sally ride, willing her to get another blue ribbon."

"Jane…" It was a breath of awed appreciation. "I'll wear it until it falls apart," he declared huskily. "It will be the most treasured possession in my wardrobe. Money can't buy what you've just given me…the time, the care, the personal thought you've put into it…"

Jane bridled with pleasure. "Well, you are going to be my brother-in-law."

"I surely am." He grinned at her. "Thank you, little sister."

She glowed with happiness.

We three are our own little family, Sally thought, and to her mind this was the happiest family Christmas she'd had. Their self-appointed Santa Claus joyously continued the bestowing of gifts—to Sally from Jack the title deeds of the property and a magnificent diamond to match her solitaire engagement ring. It hung on a fine gold chain, which she immediately fastened around her neck, loving its simplicity—something she could wear all the time instead of as a showpiece for a grand occasion.

She'd bought him a video camera for recording

the special moments in their lives from now on, and Jack immediately put it to use, shooting Jane as she finally opened her own presents, capturing her slightly embarrassed delight with Sally's gift—a range of gorgeous, sexy lingerie, bought online from Victoria's Secret—and her puzzlement over the set of keys given to her by him.

"They're the keys to an apartment I bought in your name," he explained. "It's only a short walk from North Shore Hospital where you'll be working this year and I thought you'd like your own space in Sydney."

Her jaw dropped in shock.

"It's unfurnished," he went on. "You can fit it out in whatever style pleases you and I'll give you a credit card to cover the cost."

She found her voice with difficulty. "Jack…I don't know what to say. To think I was frightened of you… frightened of what you might do to us." She shook her head. "You've done so much *for* us…"

"You can say 'thank you, big brother.' And

promise never to be frightened of me in the future."

"I never will," she declared fervently, then laughed, lighting up with joy again. "Thank you, big brother. I can also promise I'll get my diploma in midwifery this year so when you and Sally decide to start a family and she gets pregnant, you can count on me to make sure every care will be taken before and after the birth of your baby." She clapped her hands excitedly at the thought of the addition to their family. "*Our* baby!"

"Oh, Lord! Save me from the mother hen!" Sally wailed.

Which set them all off laughing.

They went into the breakfast room in high good humour, and having eaten well, Jane headed off to laze the rest of the morning away by the swimming pool, and Jack suggested he and Sally go for a stroll around the property before joining her. They set off down the maple avenue, happily hand in hand, heading for the front gate, which had always been shut to Jack while her mother was here. The thought prompted Sally into wondering how much had changed for him this past year.

"Giving all this to me…I want you to feel it's your home, as well as mine and Jane's," she pressed, glancing up hopefully, not sensing any of the old darkness in him but not certain it was completely gone. Had all the ghosts of the past been laid to rest?

"Home…" he repeated musingly, a whimsical little smile on his lips as his gaze swept slowly around the lush green pastures on either side of them. He squeezed her hand. "Home is where you are, Sally. I no longer think of this place as my father's or Lady Ellen's. It belongs to you, and you've always made me feel welcomed so I'm happy to be here."

"I'm happy to be with you, too, wherever we are, Jack," she assured him. "I don't have to stay here, you know."

He shook his head. "It feels right. I like the

sense of continuity, the sense of family with you and Jane. I now have what my father didn't give me, and I want to take it into the future with our children, Sally." His vivid blue eyes blazed with conviction. "Children who'll always know what home is because they'll always be loved by us."

"Yes. Very much loved," she agreed, her heart swelling with love for him. "We're going to have a future that will more than balance the scales, Jack."

He laughed.

No darkness.

No danger.

No devil driving him.

Their first Christmas together…peace, love, joy.

They reached the gate and turned around to look back up at the big white house on the hill. Jack released Sally's hand and lifted his arm to hug her shoulders, holding her close, remembering the bitter anger he'd felt at being denied entry to this property. It was gone now. Gone, too, was the black resentment stirred by the privileged lifestyle given to his father's adopted daughters.

The material advantages of wealth did not make up for the total lack of caring by both parents. With a cruel, tyrannical mother and a father whose approval was hard won, it was no wonder that the two girls had stuck so closely together, Sally protecting her younger sister as best she could, both of them taking comfort in each other. He was glad all that rotten negativity was over for them, glad he'd forced it into the past.

They were *his* family now.

Unimaginable a year ago.

He might have been the driving power behind making it happen, but Sally's heart had made it all viable—a heart that held the gift of love.

"You know what you've done for me, Sally?" He smiled into her eyes. "I'm not outside the gate anymore. You've brought me in from the cold."

Then he kissed her and she kissed him right back.

A long, hot kiss.

A kiss that promised a wonderful, warm future.

The scales had already been more than balanced.

On his side, they overflowed with happiness and wellbeing.

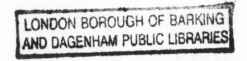

MILLS & BOON PUBLISH EIGHT LARGE PRINT TITLES A MONTH. THESE ARE THE EIGHT TITLES FOR NOVEMBER 2008.

───────── ✄ ─────────

BOUGHT FOR REVENGE, BEDDED FOR PLEASURE
Emma Darcy

FORBIDDEN: THE BILLIONAIRE'S VIRGIN PRINCESS
Lucy Monroe

HE GREEK TYCOON'S CONVENIENT WIFE
Sharon Kendrick

THE MARCIANO LOVE-CHILD
Melanie Milburne

PARENTS IN TRAINING
Barbara McMahon

NEWLYWEDS OF CONVENIENCE
Jessica Hart

THE DESERT PRINCE'S PROPOSAL
Nicola Marsh

ADOPTED: OUTBACK BABY
Barbara Hannay

MILLS & BOON®
Pure reading pleasure™

1008 Rom LP

MILLS & BOON PUBLISH EIGHT LARGE PRINT TITLES A MONTH. THESE ARE THE EIGHT TITLES FOR DECEMBER 2008.

—————— ✄ ——————

HIRED: THE SHEIKH'S SECRETARY MISTRESS
Lucy Monroe

THE BILLIONAIRE'S BLACKMAILED BRIDE
Jacqueline Baird

THE SICILIAN'S INNOCENT MISTRESS
Carole Mortimer

THE SHEIKH'S DEFIANT BRIDE
Sandra Marton

WANTED: ROYAL WIFE AND MOTHER
Marion Lennox

THE BOSS'S UNCONVENTIONAL ASSISTANT
Jennie Adams

INHERITED: INSTANT FAMILY
Judy Christenberry

THE PRINCE'S SECRET BRIDE
Raye Morgan

MILLS & BOON®
Pure reading pleasure™

1108 Re